NOWHERE TO TURN

YOUNG HEROES OF HISTORY

by
Alan N. Kay

W̄M KIDS WHITE MANE KIDS
SHIPPENSBURG, PENNSYLVANIA

This book is a work of historical fiction. Names, characters, places, and incidents are products of the author's imagination and are based on actual events.

Map drawn by author.

This White Mane Books publication
was printed by
Beidel Printing House, Inc.
63 West Burd Street
Shippensburg, PA 17257-0708 USA

The acid-free paper used in this book meets the guidelines for permanence and durability of the Committee on Production Guide-lines for Book Longevity of the Council on Library Resources.

For a complete list of available publications
please write
White Mane Books
Division of White Mane Publishing Company, Inc.
P.O. Box 708
Shippensburg, PA 17257-0708 USA

Library of Congress Cataloging-in-Publication Data

Kay, Alan N., 1965-
    Nowhere to turn : young heroes of history / by Alan N. Kay.
        p. cm. -- (White Mane kids)
    Summary: In 1862, having left his uncle's farm in Pennsylvania to join the Union
Army, twelve-year-old Thomas experiences the bloody horror of the Battle of Antietam.
    Includes bibliographical references.
    ISBN 1-57249-297-X (alk. paper)
        1. Antietam, Battle of, Md., 1862--Juvenile fiction. [1.Antietam, Battle of, Md.,
1862--Fiction. 2. United States--History--Civil War, 1861-1865--Fiction.] I. Title. II.
WM kids.

PZ7.K178 No 2002
[Fic]--dc21
                                                                2002016871

PRINTED IN THE UNITED STATES OF AMERICA

This book is dedicated to the many mascots that have served our country in times of war. Their loyalty and sacrifices were a service we should never forget. May they rest in peace.

Contents

CHARACTERS

Thomas Adams—our main character. He is a 12-year-old Irish boy living with his uncle's family in the countryside near Philadelphia, Pennsylvania.

Thomas' Family

Mary—his oldest sister, age 13

Helen—his youngest sister, age 8

David—his 15-year-old brother, who has disappeared

Joshua, Zachary, Ethan, Rachel, and Jamie—Thomas' cousins

Uncle Robert and Aunt Patricia—parents of Joshua, Zachary, Ethan, Rachel, and Jamie

Alfie—Thomas' first dog

Blue—the regimental dog

Joey, Peter, and Bobby—the neighborhood bullies

Taylor—Joey, Peter, and Bobby's dog

Mark and Chris—friends of Thomas' in the regiment

Characters Based on Soldiers in the Union or Confederate Army

Senator Edward Baker—founder of the 71st Pennsylania Volunteer Infantry, the California Regiment

Colonel Isaac Wistar—Senator Baker's second in command

General George B. McClellan—overall Union commander of the Army of the Potomac

General Robert E. Lee—overall Confederate commander of the Army of Northern Virginia

Familiar Vocabulary of the Civil War Era

Secession—the withdrawal of a state from the Federal Union

Confederacy (also Confederate States of America)—the name adopted by the government of 11 slaveholding Southern states of the United States that seceded from the Union

Abolitionist—a person who actively tries to end slavery through speeches, writings, or actions

Preface

What is historical fiction and who are the *Young Heroes of History?*

Young Heroes of History focuses on children and young adults who were heroes in their time. Although they may not have achieved fame or fortune, they made a difference in the lives of those near to them. Many were strong in body and spirit, but others managed to do the best they could in the time and place in which they lived.

Although the heroes of this series are fictional, these young Americans are placed in situations that were very real. The events of the time period as well as many of the people in these stories are accurately based on the historical records. Sometimes the language and actions of the people may be hard to understand or may seem inappropriate, but this was a different time.

Introduction

Thomas Adams lived on a farm in Pennsylvania with his aunt, uncle, and cousins. Life was boring and he hated it. All he did was chore after chore and he never had any time to play or even go to school. The only friend he had was his little dog, Alfie, who would follow him wherever he went. But even Alfie was unable to stop the local boys from making fun of Thomas. They were all bigger than Thomas and their dog was mean and nasty. Whenever they found Thomas alone, they would tease and taunt him. Sometimes they would chase Thomas and Alfie all the way home.

Thomas thought when the war came that it was his chance to get away from it all. He thought it would be glorious and fun. When he saved a beautiful dog from a rushing carriage, he thought he had finally found the perfect pet. The regiment even made the dog their mascot. Thomas had finally found a home—until the first battle.

Thomas never thought that he would run. He never imagined his own regiment would try to kill him. He especially never imagined that life would be worse than it had been before joining the army.

When General Lee and the Army of Northern Virginia invaded the North, Thomas was called upon to forget his fears and help save the country. In a small town called Sharpsburg, which bordered Antietam Creek, a battle would be fought that would determine the outcome of the war and the future of the millions of slaves living in the Confederacy. Would Thomas fight? Would he run? Would he even survive?

Thomas' home near Philadelphia, and the location of the Battle of Antietam

Chapter One

Picked On

Thomas looked up from his book. The wind was blowing softly, the sky was a crystal blue, and the grass swayed gently back and forth. It was another beautiful spring day in Pennsylvania.

He looked back down again at the book in his hand. It was the third time he had read *Moby Dick* and even though it was almost better this time around, he was getting bored and stiff from lying in the grass for so long.

"Ohhhhh," he sighed deeply as he rolled his eyes and looked over at his dog, Alfie, who was curled up next to him. "When is something going to happen?"

Alfie lifted his head up from the grass and stared at Thomas. He was an ugly little dog—part spaniel, part poodle, part Labrador, and several other parts no one could identify. His curly black fur was soft in some areas but was rough and short where it had suddenly gone white. His tail was not very long and it wasn't really curled either. Like the rest of the dog, it seemed to have no idea what it was.

Thomas had found the dog sitting in the hay out-side their farm one day. Thomas' older cousin, Joshua, wanted to chase it away but Thomas and his sister, Mary, wouldn't let him. They had always wanted a dog but were unable to have one when they had lived in Boston. Now that their uncle had taken them to live in the country it seemed only natural to have a dog to play with, watch the house, and help out on the farm. Unfortunately, Alfie wasn't much help. Uncle Robert had tried to get rid of the dog but all of the kids, even Joshua, had somehow grown to love Alfie and his sad, brown eyes. Besides, they had never found his original owner, and no one in the town would have taken him anyway.

Thomas rubbed the top of Alfie's head behind the ears. "It is soooo boring around here," he said more to himself than to the dog. Alfie made no response, how-ever, he just kept wagging his tail and sticking his tongue out. "All we ever do are chores," Thomas con-tinued. "There are no games to play, no stores to go to, and not even any schools. Heck, I'd probably look for-ward to another one of Mrs. Dougherty's boring lec-tures back in Boston right about now."

"Hey, city mouse," a voice called.

Oh no, Thomas thought to himself without even turning his back. *It's Joey again. How'd he find me? And why hadn't Alfie smelled them coming? Stupid dog.*

"Hey, city mouse!" Joey called again. "You finish your chores?"

"Doubt it," another boy said laughing. "He prob-ably snuck out again to read his stupid book."

Thomas turned around to see Joey, Bobby, and Peter walking towards him. Ever since his family had moved to Frankford last year, these three boys had been picking on him. They seemed to think that it was their job to make Thomas' life miserable. No matter where he went, the boys always found him. They would chase him, beat him, and steal his things. Thomas had no idea why they hated him so much. It had to be more than that he was no good at farm chores or that he was Irish. They seemed to just take pleasure in being mean.

Thomas stood up to go.

"Hey, where you going so fast?" Joey said as he and the others approached Thomas. They had their large guard dog, Taylor, with them and he looked even meaner than usual today. "We just got here."

"Whatcha reading, city mouse?" Peter joked, grabbing the book out of Thomas' hands and staring at the cover. "Something about a whale?"

"Yes," Thomas answered sharply, grabbing the book back and sticking it under his armpit. "I'm surprised you can read it."

"Watch your tongue, mouse," Joey warned. "You ought to know better than to talk like that to us."

"I could tell what it was by the picture," Peter interrupted. "I don't need to read. It's just a waste of time anyhow."

"That's right," Bobby agreed. "What's reading ever gotten you, mouse, other than in trouble?"

"It's better than sitting on the fence chewing hay all day," Thomas answered.

"What's that supposed to mean?" Joey asked angrily. He let go of his dog a little and smiled as it growled at Thomas.

"N-nothing," Thomas said nervously. He looked down at the dog and remembered how he had seen it chase and destroy a rabbit one day. It took pleasure in making animals and people afraid, and Thomas was no exception. He took a step back.

"You think you're better than us cuz we can't read," Joey snarled. He took another step closer to Thomas.

"N-n-no I don't," Thomas answered, taking two more steps back. He was starting to shake inside thinking about that large orange mass of fur tackling him and chomping on his leg.

"Where you going, mouse?" Joey smiled. "You afraid of my dog?"

"Just keep him away," Thomas begged as he stared down at the snarling dog. Its forehead was wrinkled in anger and saliva dripped from his teeth onto the grass.

"He won't hurt you," Joey laughed. "He just wants to play, don't ya, Taylor?"

The dog barked viciously several times.

"Ahhhh," Thomas cried as he turned and ran as fast as he could. The boys all laughed and looked down at Taylor, who was still growling.

"Get him, boy!" Joey said eagerly as he let go of the leash and watched the dog fly after Thomas.

"Ahhhhh!" Thomas screamed, looking behind him to see the dog hot on his trail. Taylor's jaws were wide open and his fur blew in the wind. Thomas ran faster.

"Ruff, ruff, ruff, ruff!" the dog barked, getting closer by the second. Thomas could almost feel the heat from the dog's breath on his back. He looked ahead. There were only grass and trees in the distance. There was nowhere to run and nowhere to hide. Taylor barked again. He would be on Thomas in a few seconds.

"Noooo," Thomas cried. "Stay back! Stay back!" He looked behind the dog. Joey and the others were standing still with their arms crossed, watching the "fun." Thomas stumbled and fell. Taylor barked and lunged at him.

"Ruff, ruff, ruff!" Alfie suddenly cried in a high-pitched voice. He jumped in front of Thomas and warned off the larger dog with a few snarls and a glimmer of teeth.

"Rrrrrrrrrrrrr," Taylor growled, stopping hard and looking the small dog over. Alfie took a step back. He was no match for Taylor.

"Ruff, ruff!" Alfie barked again.

"R-r-r-ruff," Taylor's deeper, menacing bark returned.

"Ruff," Alfie replied one last time.

Taylor jumped at Alfie. His jaws snapped at empty air as the little dog jumped out of the way and began barking and circling the frustrated Taylor.

"No, Alfie!" Thomas warned.

But it was too late. A second later, Taylor lunged at Alfie, catching him by surprise and knocking him down. The two dogs wrestled and knocked each other about while their jaws snapped in the air trying to grab a leg, an ear, or a neck.

"No, Alfie!" Thomas cried again. It was no use. The two dogs were fighting furiously trying to bite, claw, or scratch each other. For a few seconds, Alfie was able to keep out of Taylor's grasp by dodging back and forth and one time he even scooted under Taylor's legs. Then, Taylor's large foreleg caught Alfie right in the jaw and knocked him down.

"Alfie!" Thomas yelled.

Alfie shook his head and looked up to see Taylor jumping at him again. He dodged to the side and then, instead of running further back, he bit Taylor as hard as he could in the neck.

Taylor screamed in pain. The cut wasn't deep enough to do any real damage, but it set Taylor into a rage. He rushed Alfie, biting and barking and knocking the little black dog down with the force of his larger body. His jaws clamped down on Alfie's right hind leg.

"Raaaaahhh," Alfie cried. Taylor took a step back and prepared to jump at Alfie again.

"Stop!" a voice screamed. It was Mary, Thomas' older sister. She had thrown up her right hand and jumped in between the two dogs. "Stop right now!" she yelled again at the big angry dog.

Taylor didn't move. Instead, he growled at Mary and barked angrily.

"Mary!" Thomas called out in an expression of relief and frustration. Even though Mary was only 1 year older than Thomas, it always seemed that she was coming to his rescue. He loved her dearly, but it really embarrassed him how she always had to save him in front of the boys. "Get out of the way. He'll bite you."

"Stop," Mary repeated, ignoring Thomas' warning. "Leave that little dog alone."

Taylor still growled at Mary and looked as if he was about to lunge again.

"That's enough, boy," Joey suddenly commanded, grabbing Taylor's collar and holding him tight. "You've had enough excitement for one day."

"Excitement?" Mary yelled. "Excitement? Attacking a poor defenseless dog that's half the size of your own is exciting?"

"It never would have happened," Joey answered simply, "if your baby brother hadn't run off and spooked my dog."

"I didn't spook your dog!" Thomas yelled back.

"You did too," Joey said in a calm voice. "You ran so fast he got all excited. He just thought you were playing."

"You sicked him on me!" Thomas cried out.

"Oh come on, mouse," Joey said in a doubtful tone. "Would I really do a thing like that, Mary?" Joey went on, turning his attention to Thomas' older sister. "Do you really think I would purposefully let my dog attack someone?"

"I certainly do," Mary shot back. "You've been picking on Thomas ever since we moved here."

"No I haven't," Joey replied. "We've just been having some fun."

"Fun?" Mary said, turning her attention to Alfie, who was still lying on the grass. "Fun? Look what you've done to our dog." She held up Alfie's leg that was still bleeding.

"Hey, your dog started it," Joey answered defensively. He realized that he could get in trouble if people thought his dog was really dangerous. "My dog was just playing with Thomas when that little black ball jumped up and started the fight."

"That's not what happened at all," Thomas said as he moved to join Mary at Alfie's side.

"It sure is," Joey argued. "And I got witnesses to prove it. Right guys?"

Bobby and Peter nodded their heads in agreement. "Right," they said together.

"Forget them," Mary said to Thomas. "We need to get Alfie home." She carefully picked up the dog and began to stand.

"Hope your dog's alright," Joey called as the two walked away with Alfie.

"Jerks," Mary said under her breath. She turned and saw the boys smiling and laughing. "C'mon, Thomas," she went on as she turned back and headed home. "Let's go."

Chapter Two

The Cousins

Thomas slammed the door open and cleared the way for Mary.

"Over here," Thomas urged. "Put him on the table."

"What's going on?" Thomas' older cousin, Joshua, asked. He had been surprised by their sudden entry and almost spilled the milk he was drinking. "What happened?"

"Get some bandages from the cabinet." Mary commanded Thomas. She ignored Joshua's question completely and laid Alfie down on top of the table. "And get a bucket and some clean water!" she shouted.

"Mary, what is going on?" Joshua shouted as he stood up and made his way to the table. "What happened to Alfie?"

"He was in a fight," Mary answered simply. She grabbed the washcloth Thomas handed her and began cleaning Alfie's leg. "We've got to stop the bleeding," she said to both of them. "Joshua, take the cloth and put pressure on his leg, right there."

"But," Joshua protested.

"Do it!" Mary commanded. "Thomas, get some more bandages. His leg is worse than I thought."

"Would someone please explain what is going on," Joshua begged. He had taken the washcloth and was holding it down on Alfie's leg while he turned his head to talk to Mary and Thomas.

"Hey, what's all the shouting about?" Joshua's brother Ethan wondered aloud as he came into the room. Although Ethan was the youngest of Joshua's brothers, he was still 4 years older than Thomas. Those 4 years made him the bossiest of all of Thomas' cousins since he had no one younger to push around except Thomas.

"Alfie's been hurt," Joshua answered.

"Wow," Ethan whistled. "Is he going to be alright?"

"I don't know yet," Mary answered abruptly as she turned and left the room.

"Mom, Mom!" Ethan turned and shouted towards the outside, "come quick."

Ethan ran out the door yelling for his mother, his other brother Zachary, or anyone else he could think of. Joshua shook his head back and forth in disgust.

"He's such a big mouth," Joshua groaned.

"Has the bleeding stopped?" Mary asked when she returned with more water. She pushed Joshua aside and inspected Alfie's wound.

"It's still bleeding a little," she mumbled, taking Joshua's hand and returning it to its spot on Alfie's leg. "Keep putting on pressure." Mary turned away again.

"Mary!" Joshua shouted, grabbing her dress with his free hand and stopping her in her tracks, "tell me what's happening?"

"Alfie was attacked by another dog," Mary answered.

"What dog?" Mary's Aunt Patricia interrupted as she walked into the house followed by Ethan, his brother Zachary, and their younger sisters, Rachel and Jamie.

"Taylor," Mary answered pulling Joshua's hand off her clothes.

"Taylor?" Zachary repeated. "You mean Joey's dog?"

"Yes," Mary answered. "That big bully was picking on Thomas again."

"I'm sure Thomas did something to start it," Joshua commented.

"You're always taking Joey's side," Thomas complained bitterly as he walked back into the room with the bandages.

"No I'm not," Joshua argued.

"Are too!" Thomas shouted back.

"Am not," Joshua answered.

"Quiet, you two," Aunt Patricia commanded as she approached the table. "This is no time for an argument."

"Sorry, mom," Joshua apologized.

"Fine," his mother acknowledged, "now move your hand and let me look at the wound."

"I'm taking care of it, Auntie," Mary protested. She hated how her aunt treated her like a child all of the time. Aunt Patricia always favored her own daughters even though Mary was clearly smarter and harder working than either Rachel or Jamie.

"The bite is all the way down to the bone," Aunt Patricia said to no one in particular, ignoring Mary completely. "And I think it may be broken as well."

"Broken?" Thomas cried. "Oh no!"

"Don't worry," Rachel offered. "Mom will fix it fine. Right, Mom?"

"I'll try, honey," Aunt Patricia answered. "Mary, put that water down and get me something I can use for a splint."

"But," Mary began.

"Now!" her aunt yelled.

Mary turned in a huff and stormed out the door. It happened again. Her aunt came in, took over, and treated Mary like a slave. *When would it end?* she cried to herself.

"What did you do to make Joey angry?" Ethan asked Thomas as he watched his mother begin to wrap Alfie's leg.

"I didn't do anything!" Thomas yelled in frustration. "He started picking on me."

"Yeah, sure he did," Joshua added. "We all know what a nuisance you can be."

"Shut up!" Thomas yelled as he punched Joshua in the stomach. "You guys are always taking his side and I'm sick of it."

"You little jerk," Joshua swore as he grabbed Thomas and swung him to the ground.

"I'm not little!" Thomas yelled back. He stood back up and rushed Joshua, sending the two of them into the chairs next to the table. Joshua was caught off guard and unable to pull Thomas off him. Thomas may have been much smaller than Joshua, but his anger and energy held Joshua back. He tried, but couldn't get any leverage against his angry little cousin.

"I'll show you," Thomas went on. He was so sick of the way his cousins treated him. Ever since his older brother David ran away, there had been no one left in the family for Thomas to play with. It seemed as if Aunt Patricia's kids resented Thomas, Mary, and their little sister, Helen. Perhaps it was because when they lived in Boston, they would go to school to learn while Joshua, Ethan, and Zachary spent their childhood working. Whatever the reason, they made Thomas feel like an unwanted guest.

"Stop it right now, you two," Aunt Patricia screamed. "How am I supposed to fix this poor dog's leg with the two of you making all this noise?"

Both boys stopped immediately and looked over at the table where Alfie was still lying quietly.

"Sorry, mom," Joshua said.

"Sorry, Aunt Patricia," Thomas said, getting up off Joshua and turning away. "It's just that—"

"I don't want to hear it, Thomas," Aunt Patricia interrupted him. "I'm sick of how you always fight with my boys. Now go outside and help your sister find me a splint."

Thomas opened his mouth to protest but realized it would do no good. He turned and headed towards the door, listening to the boys chuckling softly as he went.

"Arrrgghhh," he groaned once he was outside. "I hate them. I hate them all!"

"I know how you feel," Mary said standing by the fence. She was breaking off a small piece of it to use as a splint for Alfie. "They all treat us so unfair—Aunt Patricia, Joshua, Zachary, Ethan, and especially prissy Rachel and Jamie. I don't think we'll ever get treated fairly in this house."

"Why do they hate us so much?" Thomas wondered.

"I don't know," Mary answered. "Maybe they don't like having to take care of us. Ever since mom and dad

died, they've gotten no money or help from anyone.
Then when Grampa threw us out of the apartment in
Boston and we had to move here, they blamed it all on
us."

"Maybe they're mad cuz dad was involved with
that whole John Brown thing," Thomas suggested.

"Maybe," Mary said.

"I sure wish David were here," Thomas complained.
"At least then there would be someone to beat up on
Joshua for me."

"All David ever did was cause more trouble," Mary
answered.

"Yeah," Thomas agreed. "But it still was fun watching him beat up on Joshua."

"Yeah," Mary smiled, remembering the family wrestling matches on the apartment floor in Boston. "C'mon,
let's give this splint to Aunt Patricia."

CHAPTER THREE

FORT SUMTER

Aunt Patricia had finally finished setting the splint and they were all sitting quietly, patting Alfie and trying to comfort him.

"Good boy," Thomas whispered quietly, scratching Alfie gently behind the ears.

"Poor thing," Rachel said softly, rubbing Alfie's tummy.

The door slammed open, smashing into the wooden wall and startling everyone.

"By God they've done it!" cried Uncle Robert as he burst into the crowded room.

All heads turned towards the door. Even Alfie lifted his head slightly at the sound of Uncle Robert's voice. They all knew how worried he had been. Hardly any work was getting done around the farm while they all waited for news from the papers. Indeed, Uncle Robert had been out all day again, trying to get more information about the problems in South Carolina. Even though it really didn't affect their life on the farm, everyone wanted to know if there really would be a war, or if President Lincoln would simply let the

15

Southerners leave the United States of America and form their own government.

Uncle Robert looked down at everyone, panting deeply as he tried to catch his breath. He was a large man, both in height and in build. His thick black beard and rosy round face sat atop a firm, rugged body. His muscles pushed at the seams of his old farm clothes, and his deep burly voice vibrated through everyone's bones. He commanded respect and awe especially from his young nephew, Thomas, who worshiped him. Uncle Robert was the only one who didn't pick on Thomas. On hot summer days, while sitting under the big oak tree, Thomas would often imagine his tall, powerful uncle running to his rescue, pushing people out of the way and throwing Joey, Bobby, and Peter around like twigs.

Yet Uncle Robert never came to Thomas' rescue. He hardly noticed him at all. When the boys chased Thomas, it was always Mary who scared them off by yelling and screaming at the top of her lungs. That only made Thomas feel worse. No one seemed to care, not even his uncle.

"Done what, Uncle Robert?" Thomas quickly asked. Thomas was always the first one in the house to show an interest in the news. Part of the reason was because his own father and mother had exposed him to so many experiences when they lived in Boston. His mother, Regina, a teacher, had often gone to the abolitionist meetings at the local church. The group discussed how they could get the government to outlaw slavery. His father, Jonathan, had also taken an active part in the organization. One time they even had a fugitive slave hiding in their house for several nights.

Thomas also was interested in the news because it made his uncle notice him. With his parents dead and his older cousins resenting him, the only people who seemed to like him were his sisters, Mary and Helen. But they were girls and Thomas wanted a boy to talk to or better yet, a man like his Uncle Robert.

"The Carolinians have attacked the Federal troops stationed at Fort Sumter," Uncle Robert exclaimed as he paced around the room, waving his hands and looking at his three sons, his wife, his two daughters, and finally at Thomas. "They attacked Fort Sumter, can you believe it? Are they crazy? They've started a war! A war! Those idiots, those fools! Don't they realize what they've done?"

"Are you sure, Dad?" Joshua asked.

"Of course I'm sure," he answered gruffly.

"Wow," Zachary whistled.

Everyone sat quietly for a moment. Only Helen seemed undisturbed by the news as she continued rubbing Alfie's fur.

"They've done it...they've gone and done it!" Ethan yelled as he pushed his chair out from under him and stood up. "Can you believe it? War!"

"Who do you think will win?" Zachary joined in.

"Who'll go fight?" Rachel wondered aloud.

"Think they'll call for us?" Joshua suggested.

"If they do, we'll show 'em how an Adams fights," Zachary boasted.

"Yeah, you bet," Ethan agreed.

"We'll show 'em," Joshua added as he too stood up and grabbed his brothers by the arms. Then he pushed the two together and shortly the boys were on the floor wrestling.

"Boys, boys, cut that out," their mother yelled. "We don't know that there will be a war and we certainly don't know if they'll call for volunteers, especially boys! Robert, don't you think you're exaggerating?"

"Absolutely not," he replied. "Now that the Carolinians have fired on a United States fort, there's no way Lincoln will just sit around. He has to do something."

"Well even if he does, don't you think it will be over before next year?" Aunt Patricia asked.

"Well, sure. Them rebels don't stand a chance against the United States Government," Uncle Robert replied. "Just like the Indians and the Mexicans, those boys will be licking their wounds soon enough."

"And it'll be over?" Thomas wondered aloud.

"No, not that quickly," Uncle Robert replied. "They still got to figure out what to do after. Them Southerners aren't going to change their ways so fast. Lincoln's probably going to have to punish them. And then there's the matter of the slaves? No one knows what he's going to do about them."

"Why, he'll set them free of course!" Mary interrupted. As Thomas' sister she too had been exposed to even more of their parents' abolitionist ideas. She hated slavery more than she hated her life on the farm. Indeed, Thomas had never seen her face as bright and red as when she began to preach about the evils of slavery. "He has to. Don't you see, it's what this whole war is about."

"I ain't going to fight to free no slaves," Zachary butted in.

"Yeah, I'm going to defend my country," said Joshua.

"And I'm going to whip some rebel butt!" laughed Ethan.

"Now boys," Uncle Robert began patiently, "as your mother says, we don't know who'll be going to fight or when or if. But you are right about one thing, this war is not about slavery. That was your Uncle John's idea. He's the one who went off all crazy with that abolitionist junk."

"Oh Robert, are we going to have this discussion again?" Patricia asked with a look of annoyance and a gasp of air. "Every time we've discussed this, we've argued."

"I know, I know," he answered with a wave of his hand. "You say that John was just trying to do what was right, and I say he was a crazy idiot. Then I yell, then you yell, and we argue and go in circles but never get anywhere. But I'll tell you one thing, the boys who volunteer to fight will be fighting for the Union. They'll be fighting to keep this country together and protect the only true land of freedom on the face of the earth. No matter how much them abolitionists want to make this their personal crusade to free the slaves, these boys won't be going to fight for no black people. Heck, if they really cared so much for the slaves then we would have had a war a long time ago!"

"Well, we should have had a war to free the slaves," cried Mary. "Slavery is the most vile thing on the face of this earth and I don't know how—"

"Now you hush, young lady," Uncle Robert interrupted with his sternest, deepest voice possible. His anger was beginning to build and as he talked, his voice grew louder and louder. "I'm tired of listening to your preaching. You, your daddy, and the rest of them abolitionists, like John Brown, would have all of us kill each other for them Africans. Free the slaves, free the slaves, you all cry. But it's never as easy as that. What do we do once they're freed? They have no money, no homes, no education. And what of the Southerners who all of a sudden have no labor to work their farms? What of the poor Southerner who has to find a job when there are all of these new people competing for jobs? You don't think about all the issues involved. You just preach and rant and rave and I am tired of it. I will fight and die for this country and for the freedom it represents, but I will not hear any more nonsense from you. Is that understood?"

Mary looked down at the table. She didn't dare face her uncle. His face was beet red and his breathing was coming in huge gasps. She had never seen him this angry.

There was silence for several minutes as Uncle Robert's anger slowly subsided.

"Aw heck," he said with a huge sigh once the anger was gone. He felt drained from all of the excitement. "I don't know what I'm saying. It don't matter anyhow. I'm tired of arguing with you and I'm tired of this whole fight. Patricia," he said turning towards her, "if there is a call for volunteers, I'm going."

"What?" Patricia exclaimed. "So soon? What about the farm?"

"It will be fine for a couple of months," Robert answered simply.

"I'm going too, Father!" Joshua quickly added.

"Me too!" shouted Zachary.

"Don't leave me out!" added Ethan.

"Yeah, me too!" Thomas enthusiastically shouted.

"Now wait just a minute, boys," Uncle Robert began with a wave of his hand. "You are all old enough to go off to war and it would make me proud to see you acting and fighting like men, but Thomas, you're gonna have to stay. Your cousins are much older. Joshua and Zachary here are 17 and 18 while Ethan's almost fully grown at 16. But you're just a boy, a big boy I'll admit. Heck, you're almost as tall as Ethan and you run as fast as your dad, but you're still only 12."

"But Uncle...," Thomas whimpered.

"Besides," his uncle continued as if he didn't even hear, "we need somebody to stay home with the women. Your aunt is more than capable of running this household, and your cousins Rachel and Jamie and your sister Mary will lend a hand, but I still would like to have one boy at home just in case."

"But Uncle...," Thomas whimpered again.

"No, Thomas, that's final. And it's final for the rest of you. Clear out of the house and start your evening chores. Your mother and I need to talk. Now skit!"

With some mumbling and moaning, Zachary, Joshua, Ethan, Mary, Thomas, Rachel, Jamie, and little Helen all dragged their feet slowly out the door.

Chapter Four

Volunteers Needed

"C'mon, Alfie," Thomas urged his dog. "You can do it."

Alfie looked up nervously. His sad brown eyes looked close to tears as he softly whimpered and hobbled on his bandaged hind leg. It had been almost a month since the fight with Taylor and Alfie's leg showed no signs of healing. Mary said that Aunt Patricia had set it wrong and that Alfie would never run again, but Thomas refused to believe that. He figured Mary said that because she was angry at Aunt Patricia for taking over.

"Keep trying," Thomas said softly. "It will get better soon."

"Maybe he needs crutches," an approaching voice called from behind. Laughter immediately followed and Thomas knew it had to be Joey, Bobby, and Peter again.

"Leave me alone, you guys," Thomas snapped angrily as he turned to face the three boys. He let out a small sigh of relief when he noticed that Joey's dog, Taylor, was not with them. "I don't need any hassles from you today."

"What makes you think we're going to give you any hassles?" Joey asked innocently. "We just came by to see how your dog was doing."

"As if you care," Thomas said bitterly.

"We do," Joey claimed with a sincere look on his face. "Right guys?"

"Yeah, of course, we do," Peter agreed.

"We feel bad for the little guy," Bobby added.

"You do?" Thomas asked in disbelief.

"Sure," Joey insisted. "If he doesn't get any better, Taylor will have to go back to chasing rabbits."

The boys all exploded in laughter. Thomas' heart sank as he realized yet again what jerks they were.

"Get out of here," Thomas cried as he swung his fist at Joey and hit only air. "Leave me alone."

"H-hey, h-hey," Joey said in between laughs as he continued to dodge Thomas' haphazard punches. "I was only joking."

"I don't care," Thomas said angrily. "I'm tired of you three."

"Hey, what's going on?" a deep voice asked from behind.

"Hey, Josh," Joey answered as he saw Thomas' older cousin approaching. "We just came by to check out how your dog was doing."

"Well, that's real nice of you," Josh replied. "But how come Thomas is swinging at you."

"Oh, you know your kid cousin," Joey answered quickly before Thomas could say anything. "He's always overreacting."

"I am not!" Thomas shouted. "You guys were making fun of Alfie."

"Oh, lay off it, Thomas," Joshua scolded him. "I ain't got time for this. I'm going into town to see if there is any news about regiments forming. I heard that any day now they're going to be looking for volunteers to sign up. Hey," Josh turned suddenly to the three boys, "you guys wanna come with me? I bet you could sign up if you fudged your age a little."

"M-maybe later," Joey said quickly and nervously. "My dad wants me home soon. Just let me know how it goes."

"Yeah, me too," Peter added.

"See ya!" Bobby said with a wave of his hand.

The boys turned and quickly headed away from the confused Thomas and Joshua.

"What was that all about?" Joshua wondered aloud.

"They seemed scared to me," Thomas suggested.

"Hmmm," Joshua thought. "Nahh, they must just be in a hurry."

"They never seem interested in the news," Thomas added quickly. He wanted to try to get Joshua angry at them, so that he wouldn't always take their side. "Every time I talk about you and Uncle Robert joining up, they get all funny and start picking on me."

"That's cuz you're Thomas," Joshua said as if that explained everything. "They always act that way with you."

"Yeah but...," Thomas tried to argue.

"I gotta go," Joshua cut him off. He turned and headed into town. "Oh," he said as he stopped walking and turned back towards Thomas, "I almost forgot, Dad wants to talk to you."

"Oh great," Thomas mumbled. "What's he want now?"

"Thomas!" Uncle Robert's voice thundered across the open fields. "Thomas Adams! Where are you?"

He sounds angry, Thomas thought to himself. *What did I forget to do now?*

"Thomas!" Uncle Robert repeated.

"Over here!" Thomas answered as he walked towards his uncle. "I was just taking Alfie out for a walk."

"Stop worrying about that dog," Uncle Robert scolded. "I told you to clear out the grass behind the shed over an hour ago."

"But I did," Thomas whined.

"You call that clear?" Uncle Robert said angrily, pointing towards the field in a sweeping motion. "There are still twigs everywhere and I already lifted up three large rocks while I was waiting for you."

"Ohhhhhh," Thomas moaned.

"If I have to tell you one more time to repeat another chore," Uncle Robert went on, "I swear I will take that dog and send him away."

"I'm sorry," Thomas said automatically. He knew his uncle didn't really mean it. He had been threatening to do that for over a year now and not once had he even come close. By now Thomas knew to stop arguing with him and to let him just go on until he was done.

"You're always sorry," Uncle Robert went on. "You say you'll do better next time and then you go and do the same thing all over again."

Thomas did not say a word. He just quietly walked with his head down past his uncle and started to clean up the field.

"Every time I tell you to clean up," his uncle droned on, "you go out there and do it quickly."

Thomas had stopped listening completely, but he continued to shake his head so that his uncle thought he was paying attention.

"And I mean it this time!" Uncle Robert finally finished and stormed away.

"Thank God," Thomas sighed. He bent down and picked up another twig and threw it as far as he could. Then he picked up another and another and threw them anywhere too. He looked down at the rocks his uncle had mentioned and kicked them around in the dirt so that no one could see them. Then he walked all around the field, scuffing his feet and moving the twigs and rocks around enough to hide them from his uncle.

"That's good enough," Thomas sighed after a few minutes of work. "I'm tired."

He turned and headed for the big oak tree at the edge of the field. "C'mon, Alfie," he said.

A little while later, Mary came by.

"Whatya doing?" she asked politely.

"Nothing," Thomas answered as he picked up another blade of grass and began to slowly pick it apart.

"Can I join you?" Mary asked.

"Sure," Thomas shrugged. "It's not my tree."

"Thanks," Mary said as she patted her dress under the back of her legs and sat next to Thomas. "Was that Joey I saw over here earlier?" she began.

"Yeah," Thomas mumbled.

"What did he want?" Mary asked.

"To cause trouble as usual," Thomas replied in an annoyed voice.

"Did he say anything about the fight with his dog?" Mary wondered curiously. She still found it hard to believe how cruel and careless boys could be. Even

Thomas sometimes was mean to her. He was usually a great little brother but whenever he was around the older boys he would make fun of her and talk down to her just to impress them. It drove Mary crazy and she swore that one day she was going to let Thomas fend for himself and watch as those bullies beat up on him.

"He just laughed and said that Alfie needed to get better so Taylor wouldn't have to start chasing rabbits," Thomas answered.

"He said that?" Mary exclaimed. "How can he be so heartless?"

"Who cares?" Thomas mumbled in annoyance. "Who cares what Joey and the others think? They're just a bunch of jerks."

"That's for sure," Mary agreed.

"And cowards too," Thomas answered.

"Huh?" Mary wondered. "Why do you say that?"

"I think that they are afraid to join up," Thomas explained.

"For the war?" Mary said.

"Of course for the war," Thomas replied. "What else?"

"What makes you think they're afraid?"

"They're always refusing to talk about it," Thomas explained. "And when Joshua said he was going to look into joining up, they acted all funny and said they had to leave."

"That's strange," Mary commented. "Did Joshua say anything else about joining up?"

"No, he just said..."

"Pa! Pa!" a voice was shouting from down the road. Mary and Thomas looked up to see Joshua running towards them. "Pa! Pa!" he was crying at the top of his lungs as he ran. "They need us, they need us!"

"Pa!" Joshua shouted again as he neared the oak tree. He stopped, took a deep breath to slow his panting, and called to Mary and Thomas. "Have you seen Pa?"

"He's in the house," Thomas answered. "What's going on?"

"Senator Baker is forming a regiment!" Joshua exclaimed. "There is a recruitment officer in town right now and he said he wants us to sign up."

"Us?" Thomas asked eagerly. His eyes lit up and he started to stand.

"Not you, stupid," Joshua scolded. "Me and Pa and Zach and even Ethan. He said we are all needed."

"But," Thomas began as Joshua turned away, "what about me?" he said softly, sitting back down and watching Joshua run into the house. "What about me?"

Mary and Thomas sat quietly and watched the house. They could hear shouting and crying inside but had no interest in going in the house. This was Uncle Robert and his boys' celebration, not theirs.

"I'm sorry, Thomas," Mary said finally, breaking the silence. "I know how much you want to get out of here."

"It's just not fair," Thomas whined. "Why do they get to go and I don't? I'm just as big as Ethan. I can hold a gun. I can fight."

"You're just too young," Mary said even though she realized as soon as she said it that it was the wrong thing to say.

"I am not too young!" Thomas shouted, standing up. "I'm as tall as Zachary and smarter than all three of them combined."

"At least you have the possibility of leaving," Mary countered angrily. "You can run off to fight, but I can't do anything at all. I'm stuck here in this awful house with that awful Aunt and terrible cousins."

"But you're a girl," Thomas argued.

"So?" Mary snapped back.

"Girls can't fight," Thomas answered simply.

"Maybe not," Mary agreed, "but they can do more than sit around and wait for the men to come back."

"So," Thomas said simply, "do something."

"What?" Mary cried. "What can I do? Aunt Patricia has me so busy that all I ever do are chores. I'm more of a slave than a member of the family."

"Oh come on, Mary," Thomas argued. "It's not that bad."

"Yes, it is!" Mary yelled. "I have to wash the clothes and clean the furniture and wash the dishes and take care of Helen and—"

"I get the idea," Thomas interrupted her. "But I have a lot of chores to do too."

"Yeah but it's different for you," Mary replied.

"How?" Thomas asked.

"You can look forward to something when you get older," Mary explained. "You can read and learn and maybe go to some school somewhere. You can get a good job and own your own store or do whatever you want. What good is all the reading and learning I do? I can read all I want, but all I could ever do is become a teacher or a housewife."

Thomas didn't respond. She was right and there was nothing either of them could do about it. He looked down at his feet. Mary looked up at the sky in frustration. Tears started to flow slowly down her cheeks.

"I'm running away, Mary," Thomas said finally. "I'm running away to join up."

"What?" Mary exclaimed, wiping the tears from her face and turning to face Thomas. "You can't do that. Uncle Robert will never let you."

"He doesn't have to know," Thomas answered simply.

"But if he doesn't come with you, there won't be anyone to help you sign the papers," Mary protested. "As soon as they know your age they'll turn you away."

"I'll join up somewhere else," Thomas explained. "This can't be the only town that Senator Baker is recruiting out of. I'll go into the city and find some older guy to lie about my age and then join up. You know how much older I look anyway. It'll be easy."

"You can't just run away from your problems," Mary argued. She realized that Thomas' plan would work fine. There were plenty of people who would look the other way and let a kid join, especially if Thomas took a few dollars with him and paid off someone.

"Why not?" Thomas argued. "You said yourself that you wished you could get away."

"Yeah but...," Mary tried to argue.

"I'm doing it, Mary," Thomas said simply.

"But Thomas," Mary said desperately, "I'll be all alone."

"You'll have Helen," Thomas suggested.

"She's just a baby," Mary complained.

"I'm sorry, Mary," Thomas answered softly. "I have to do this. I can't stand it here."

"I know," Mary sighed softly. "I know."

"Write me?" Mary said after a few seconds of silence. She realized there was no way she could convince

Thomas to stay. Besides, she'd do the same thing if she could.

"Of course I will," Thomas said with a smile.

CHAPTER FIVE

THE LETTER

Letter #3
Thomas Adams to Mary Adams
July 1861
Dear Mary:

How are you sis? I have missed you so much here at camp. It seems like years since I left you at the farm and joined the army. I really am sorry that I had to run away like that but you know I needed to. Besides, I think this army stuff is more boring than the farm anyway.

The days seem to last forever here with no end in sight, and I often wonder what it is I have gotten myself into. All we do is drill, drill, and drill. We dig trenches, we clean our rifles, and we practice putting up and taking down tents. It all seems so silly! If we are going to war then let's get on with it already.

Yesterday all we did was march! You cannot imagine what it is like to march all day with no idea of where you are going, or when you will stop. Can you imagine having men all around you in lines so long that all you can see is the backs of their heads and their rifles sticking up? Actually, most of the time you can't even see that much because of all the dirt. When hundreds of men

32

are marching down a dirt road, the dust gets so thick that you can barely breathe. It gets in your eyes and it stings. Then, of course, there is the problem of my uniform. Since they only make a certain size, mine is all wrong. I may be big for my age but my body is still different from most of these men. My pants legs are too long, my sleeves flap around my arms, and this makes it even more difficult for the march ahead.

It is even worse for some of the older men. As you know I am one of the youngest boys in the whole regiment, although, I suspect there are several other boys who lied about their age too and, of course, there are the drummer boys. Anyway, the older men sometimes have trouble with all of the marching, the heat, and the dust, and I have seen many of them drop to the side of the road as we've plugged along.

This led to some trouble for me. As I told you in the last letter, many of the older soldiers resent my young age and like it even less when I can do all this marching and drilling better than them. Well, three days ago, this Englishman named Chester was marching right next to me, stumbling and staggering for the last mile. He kept looking at me as I marched straight and I could tell he hated seeing me do what he could not. Well, that night he decided to pick a fight with me in front of all his friends. He started cursing and calling me things like "stupid Irish fool" and "little dirtball." His friends who were all Englishmen and didn't like anything Irish, especially me, made a circle around us so no one else could see. Then the old fool started swinging and charging me but he kept missing. I think he was half drunk to begin with and his anger only made him that much worse. I thought I might actually have a chance until one of his friends tripped me and then Chester jumped on me and started to punch and kick me. It really hurt. It was nothing like when Uncle or the boys around the town used to hit me. This man was punching me with all the force of his hate. If the liquor hadn't been making him weaker, I think he would have killed me. Fortunately, the Captain heard the noise and showed up just in time. He yelled and cursed at us, but Chester's friends managed to put the blame on me and the Captain merely left us alone. I suppose Chester was content with having shown he could beat up a boy lying in the dirt because that seemed to be the end of it. He and his friends have left me alone since then.

I have not seen much of Uncle Robert or our cousins. I know that they are in my regiment, but in the confusion of the enlistment, I believe that they are in a different company. I suspect this is just as well since you told me how angry Uncle was when he found out I had signed up. Thank goodness he was too busy to try to do anything about it.

The men are all very different from each other. We seem to be from every walk of life. There are Irishmen like myself, Scots, Germans, Englishmen, and even some Jamaicans. What is funny is that even though we are called the California Regiment I have yet to see someone from California. We all seem to have different reasons for being here. Some, like myself, are here to get away from the farm and want to feel as if they are doing something important. Others are here for the adventure and still others are here for I don't know what. But they all seem to be good people. We are already like a family. At night we sing songs around the campfire like "Yankee Doodle" and "Battle Cry of Freedom." Sometimes

I get involved in a game of cards or play a game of checkers. We laugh, we joke, and we try to forget the next days' drills. It's the first time I've felt at home since David ran away.

Oh, before I forget, I must thank you again for your letters and your little care packages of food. The food here is the same every day and when you and your friends send us things like fresh baked cookies it makes the days so much brighter.

How are your friends in the society? I am so pleased that you found a way to help in the war. It sounds as if all the fund-raising you are doing for the soldiers will be really important. I just hope that it won't be needed much and all this will be over soon. I miss you so much, and believe it or not, I miss the farm. I don't miss my cousins, of course, or the work but I miss the beauty of the countryside and the sweet smell of the flowers by your garden.

How is Helen doing? I understand from your last letter that you are getting her to help you in the Soldiers' Aid Society. Is she really helping to sew? Do you think she understands my letters? Please tell her that I love her and miss her.

I must ask you, have you heard from our cousin George yet? I am quite nervous now that you have told me his letters have stopped. I think you are right that he probably is not writing because we will be at war with Virginia soon. I hope he does not decide to fight. Can you imagine if I actually saw him on the battlefield? I don't know what I would do. My first reaction would be to run up and hug him. But then, would he hug me back, or would he shoot me as I ran towards enemy lines? Well, I am sure that I will never see him even if he does join up.

I must be going now. They will be sounding Taps soon and I'll have to put out my light. As always, I will be thinking of you. Please don't worry, I promise I will come back home to you.

   All my love,
   Thomas

   P.S. Whoops I almost forgot! You won't believe what happened the other day. We were marching down the road when suddenly this dog jumped in front of one of the wagons. There were terrible noises and shouts as they tried to avoid the dog but it was too late and it got its foot run over. The other guys were going to chase it away, but I remembered what you had shown me about Alfie's leg and I knew I could fix this one. The guys didn't believe me at first, but we had nothing to lose so I fixed a splint and the dog seems to be doing fine now.

   We named him Blue and even though he's my dog, the whole company has kind of adopted him. He's like a mascot. Everyone plays with him and rubs his stomach and shares their hardtack with him. The Captain has already said it's O.K. to keep him as long as he doesn't get in the way. I think he realizes that we all need some kind of distraction to keep our minds off the war. He's a really neat dog: big and strong and really friendly. I am already playing with him all the time even though he isn't fully healed. I'm hoping to teach him all kinds of tricks over the next few months. O.K. I really have to go this time. They're yelling at me. Write back soon.

   Love again,
   Thomas

SOLDIERS TAKE A BREAK TO PLAY BASEBALL DURING THE CIVIL WAR.

Chapter Six

Betting on Blue

Thomas tossed the ball into the air, lifted his bat, then swung as hard as he could.

"Get it, Blue!" Thomas shouted to his new dog as the ball went sailing in the air towards a small grove of trees. Thomas watched the dog run after the ball and realized how nicely Blue's leg was healing. Even though he was still slightly lame, Blue ran with grace and style. Thomas could tell just how much he loved to run.

The dog was probably a cross between a German shepherd and a collie. He had the deep, dark black and brown fuzzy fur of a shepherd, but his nose was not as pointed and rough as most shepherd dogs. His eyes were gentle and his paws were extremely large for a dog his size. The only flaw that Blue seemed to have was that one of his ears was bent down while the other stood perfectly straight on his head. If it wasn't for that, some of the men had commented, he probably could have been a show dog.

Blue retrieved the ball and brought it back to Thomas.

"Thanks, boy," Thomas said as he retrieved the saliva-drenched ball from Blue's teeth. It amazed Thomas how Blue could hold a ball so tightly with his sharp teeth and never once leave a mark on the ball.

"Good boy," Thomas said, rubbing Blue's head. The dog's tail wagged back and forth as he stood directly in front of Thomas, panting slightly, and waiting for the ball to be hit again. Thomas giggled to himself, tossed the ball in the air, and smacked it again. Blue jumped up, almost did a backflip in his attempt to catch the ball, and ran after it again.

"Hey, Thomas," his new buddy Mark called from the edge of the field. He was a teenager, like Thomas, who had joined the regiment with his dad. The two of them quickly had become friends when they realized that they both loved the game of baseball. They had been playing almost every day and the only thing they would fight about was which ball to use: Thomas' or Mark's. "Come on. We're gonna play Chester's team again."

"Chester?" Thomas said with disappointment. "We just played them yesterday."

"He wants a rematch," Mark yelled. "Come on."

Thomas waited for Blue to return with the ball, took it from his mouth, and headed after Mark. "C'mon, Blue," he said. "Time to go."

The soldiers were already warming up by the time Thomas and Mark arrived. Several baseballs were being thrown back and forth while men from Chester's team were swinging bats to prepare for their turn.

The men had been playing baseball almost since the beginning of the regiment's formation. It was a very new game that had started in New York and Boston. Some of the men had never even heard of it and most

were unfamiliar with how to play it. Fortunately for
Thomas, he had spent his childhood in Boston and had
even played games on the Common with his brother
David and cousin George.

They had started just playing around in the beginning: hitting the ball, throwing it back and forth, and
running some bases. It didn't take long before the men
began to form teams and place bets on the winners.
Thomas had already won several dollars by betting on
his own team, but he was afraid that he would quickly
lose it all if he bet today.

Chester's team was excellent and they knew it.
Some of the men from New York City had played some
organized ball before the war. They had more talent
than any other team, and the only reason Thomas and
his team won yesterday was because several of
Chester's teammates were sick.

Thomas looked at Chester's team and counted.

"They're all here," he said with discouragement to
Mark.

"Yeah, I know," Mark replied. "But maybe they still
aren't feeling well. Come on, let's warm up."

Thomas threw some hardtack on the ground for
Blue to chew and headed out to the field. Blue grabbed
the hardened cracker and chomped on it with his sharp
teeth.

"Even his teeth can't break that stuff," Mark chuck-
led. "How do they expect us to eat it?"

As the game began, Thomas' team knew they were
in trouble. Chester's big hitters were back to normal as
they hit ball after ball into the outfield. By the time the
third inning started, the score was already 6-0.

"Hey, don't worry," Mark said to Thomas just before he went up to bat, "the spread is 10 for us today."

"Ten?" Thomas repeated.

"Yeah," Mark answered. "That means that even if we lose 21 to 11, we still win our money."[1]

"You mean everyone figured we would lose by that much?"

"Yup," Mark explained. "And there still were some guys from Company C who bet for Chester's team anyway. They figured we'd lose 21 to 5."

"That ain't going to happen," Thomas said firmly.

"It will if you strike out," Mark warned. "So don't mess up, I got my whole pay riding on this game."

Thomas gulped and headed towards the plate. He had bet a few dollars on this game as well but not his whole pay. He looked around at his teammates and could tell from their eyes that they had a lot of money riding on this game as well. *I better not screw up*, Thomas thought to himself.

Thomas managed to get a base hit and even made it to third, but then the next two guys struck out. By the time they reached the fifth inning, the score was already 20 to 10 and Chester's team had their best hitter on deck.

"Ruff, ruff, ruff," Blue barked from his spot on the grass. He had finally finished chomping on the hardtack and had been sitting patiently waiting for the game to end.

"Quiet, Blue," Thomas commanded from his position in the outfield. "The game's almost over."

"Ruff, ruff, ruff!" Blue barked again.

---

1. Author's note: Games were played to 21, not the nine innings of play today.

"Shut him up!" Chester yelled.

Thomas walked off the field. "Now listen, Blue," Thomas commanded, holding the dog's jaw firmly with one hand and pointing at him with the other. "You be quiet. The game is almost over and then we can play. Alright?"

Blue just looked up at Thomas with those friendly eyes. Thomas couldn't help but smile as he let go of Blue's snout and headed back onto the field. "Now you stay," Thomas commanded.

"You ready now?" Chester shouted in an annoyed voice.

"Yeah," Thomas shouted back.

The pitch was thrown, the batter swung and missed. "Steee-rike!" several of Thomas' teammates cried.

"Ruff, ruff, ruff!" Blue barked again.

"Blue, be quiet!" Thomas yelled.

"Ruff, ruff, ruff!"

"Blue!"

The dog ran out onto the field and came straight to Thomas.

"Blue!" Thomas scolded, pointing towards the side of the field. "Get off the field."

Blue ran around in circles, teasing Thomas and trying to jump out of his way whenever Thomas tried to grab him.

"Blue-oooh!" Thomas cried.

"Here, I got him," Mark interrupted as he grabbed the dog from behind. "Come on, Blue."

Mark sat Blue down on the grass and threw one of his pieces of hardtack to him.

"That should hold him to the end," Mark said as he returned to the field.

"Ready?" Chester yelled in anger.

"Yeah," Mark called. "He won't bother us again."

The pitcher threw another pitch and it sailed straight for the plate. With a large crack! the bat smashed straight into the ball sailing it far over the pitcher's head.

"Yee-hah!" Chester's team cheered.

The ball was definitely headed for home run territory. With one man on base already, that would give them over 21 runs and they would beat the spread. Thomas' heart sank. The other team cheered as the runner ran the bases.

Then, out of nowhere, Blue came streaking onto the field. Thomas and Mark yelled at him to stop but it was too late. With a high-reaching leap into the air, Blue grabbed the ball in his jaws and landed gently as a feather.

"That a way, Blue!" Thomas and Mark cheered.

"You're out!" several of Thomas' teammates called.

"No way!" Chester argued as he watched Blue return the ball to Thomas' hands. "That dog ain't on your team."

"Of course he is," Mark protested.

"Yeah, he's my dog," Thomas added.

"Look, kid," Chester said angrily, approaching Thomas and standing over him to try to frighten Thomas with his size. "You may need all the help you can get but dogs don't count."

"Why not?" Thomas said, backing up. He was not afraid of Chester anymore but he couldn't tolerate being so close to him.

"What do you mean, why not?" Chester shouted back. "He's a dog."

"Isn't he part of this regiment?" Mark interrupted.

"Yeah," said Chris, another of Thomas' teammates. "Blue helps us out all the time. He eats our food, sleeps in our tents, and even does some of the chores."

"That don't make him part of the regiment," Chester argued.

"Sure it does," several of the boys argued.

"Alright, alright," Chester shouted, putting up his arms in the air to shut up everyone. He could see that this could be an argument he just might lose and Chester hated to lose. "Listen. If you guys are so set on the idea of this dog being on your team, then let's up the ante."

Everyone looked at Chester blankly, waiting for him to explain.

"We all know the spread on the game was 10," Chester began. "And if the dog hadn't caught the ball we would have won and beat the spread."

"Yeah," a few men said slowly.

"Well then, I think we should try this," Chester explained. "Let's double all bets and replay the inning, this time it's us against the dog."

"What? No way!" Thomas' team shouted.

"You said that he's part of the regiment, right?" Chester asked slyly.

No one answered.

"Well then, here's your chance to prove it." Chester continued. "All the dog has to do is make three outs before we score and you win."

"Mark, Mark," Thomas turned to his friend and whispered eagerly into his ear. "I know Blue can do this! He and I play ball all the time. He can catch anything they throw at him, I know it!"

"I don't know, Thomas," Mark answered nervously. "Double pay is a lot of money."

"But I know he can do it," Thomas urged. "C'mon, guys," Thomas said to the rest of his team. "Let's do it. Blue can beat any of them, any time."

Everyone was quiet until Chris suddenly spoke up. He knew this was another chance for him to keep pitching. Chris loved to pitch. It was everything to him and he was really good at it. Day after day, he would pester anyone he could to stand over a makeshift plate and catch the balls Chris would throw. His baby blond hair would blow every which way in the wind and his blue eyes would light up with excitement every time he threw a strike. "O.K.," he said to Chester, "but I get to be the one to pitch."

"Sure," Chester said happily. It was obvious that he was sure he would win.

Thomas led Blue out onto the field and stood next to him. At first Chester protested that Thomas could not be out there, but once Thomas promised not to go after any balls everyone agreed. Besides, they all realized, Blue wouldn't stay out there without Thomas anyway.

The first batter stepped up to the plate. Chris prepared to pitch. He smiled one of his surefire smiles and glared his baby blues at the batter. The man was one of their better hitters but not their best. Mark and the other members of the team started to cheer.

"C'mon, Blue!"

"You can do it, Blue!"

"Good dog!"

Blue looked up at Thomas. He seemed a little confused. Chris let the pitch go and the first hit was on its way.

"Go get it, Blue," they shouted as the runner ran to first. Blue turned and ran after the ball.

"Run, boy, run!" everyone was shouting.

The runner had already made it to first and was on his way to second when Blue finally returned the ball to Thomas.

"Good boy," Thomas said slowly, feeling his heart sink. He grabbed the ball from Blue's teeth and returned it to the pitcher. "He'll never stop them," Thomas thought with dejection.

The second batter also had a good hit and now there was a man at third and at first.

Mark stepped onto the field.

"Thomas, you've gotta do something," he begged. "I'm going to lose all my money and we'll be the laughingstock of the whole regiment."

"But what?" Thomas wondered aloud. "He doesn't seem to get it."

"Throw him the ball," Mark suggested.

"Now?" Thomas wondered. "He's only 2 feet away."

"Just try it," Mark commanded.

Thomas lightly threw the ball to Blue. He caught it easily and returned it.

"Now take a step back and do it again," Mark ordered.

Again, Thomas threw the ball and Blue easily caught it and returned it.

"Keep backing up!" Mark said enthusiastically.

"Hey," Chester shouted. "You can't do that!"

"Why not?" Mark asked. "We're just taking a timeout to warm up."

"But...," Chester began.

"What's the matter?" Chris shouted from the pitcher's mound. "Afraid you'll lose?"

"Of course not," Chester said awkwardly.

Thomas continued to throw the ball up in the air to Blue and he continued to catch it until they were almost 30 feet apart.

"Now get behind the plate," Mark ordered.

"Hey, he can't do that," Chester protested again.

"Why not?" Mark asked. "He's just being the catcher."

Chester opened his mouth to say something but realized he really had no argument. Mark smiled and looked over at Chris. "Pitch it," he said.

Chris prepared to pitch the ball to the next batter. Thomas stood behind the plate and kept his eyes on Blue who was still out in the field. *Come on, Blue,* Thomas thought to himself.

The next batter popped a high fly into the air. All eyes turned to Blue as the dog ran almost casually in between first and second base and caught the ball squarely in his jaws.

"Yayyyyyyyyyyyyy!" Thomas and the rest of the team cheered. "Way to go, Blue!"

Chester scowled over at Thomas but said nothing.

"Batter up!" Thomas called eagerly.

"Hit a line drive," Chester whispered to his teammate before he made it to the plate. "The dog won't be able to catch that."

The man nodded, stepped up to the plate, and swung at the next pitch. Like a bullet from a gun, the ball sailed straight up the field in between second and third. Thomas groaned.

Then, as fast as the ball had rocketed, Blue raced in between the bases, grabbed the ball, and headed towards Thomas.

"Run, Blue, run!" everyone cheered.

The man on third was racing towards home. If he made it, the game would be over. Blue was gaining on him. His lame leg was barely noticeable as the fur on his back blew in the breeze.

"Run, Blue!"

The runner dove into the base. Dirt flew all around. The man looked up to see Thomas standing over him with the ball touching the man's shoulder. Blue wagged his tail at Thomas' side.

"You're out!" Thomas screamed.

"Yay, Blue!" everyone called. "That a way, Blue!"

Thomas' team cheered and hugged and slapped each other for a few seconds.

"There's still one more out," Chester interrupted as he stepped to the plate.

"Chester," Mark whispered to the others as they grew silent and watched. "He's their best hitter."

Thomas started to walk Blue out to the field again, then stopped and looked down in horror as he realized Blue was limping badly.

"He's hurt his leg again!" Thomas shouted to the others.

"Oh no!" Mark cried. "How bad is it?"

"I don't know," Thomas answered. "It's not bleeding or anything and he can still walk, but there's no way he could run like that again. At least not now."

"Forfeit! Forfeit!" Chester's team started to shout.

"No way!" Thomas yelled back. "There's only one out remaining and Blue still has some speed left in him."

Mark walked up to Thomas and whispered. "Thomas, he's limping," Mark said softly. It was obvious he was worried about the dog. "He's not going to stop them. He's just going to get hurt."

"He can do it," Thomas insisted.

"Thomas, don't worry about the money," Mark begged.

"It's not the money," Thomas argued. "It's a lot more than that. I'm tired of being pushed around. First, it was my cousins, then my neighbors, now that bully Chester. He's always making fun of us and bragging and boasting. I owe him one."

Mark stared at Thomas, wondering whether Thomas wasn't getting a little too upset about all of this.

"But what about Blue?" Mark asked.

"He'll be fine," Thomas assured him. "He's a smart dog. He won't run on his leg if it's too sore. All he has to do is catch the ball. There's already two outs. Just let him try. The worst that happens is that we lose."

"O.K., O.K.," Mark agreed.

Thomas walked slowly out to the field with Blue. He was definitely limping on his leg and Thomas began to wonder if maybe he was wrong about all this. He didn't want Blue to get hurt. When they reached the edge of the infield, Thomas bent down to look Blue in the eyes. "You O.K., boy?" Thomas asked.

Blue wagged his tail, stuck out his tongue, and stared at Thomas. Thomas smiled. Blue would be fine. "Come on, boy," he said, rubbing the dog behind the ears, "you can do it."

Blue wagged his tail again and let out a bark as Thomas returned to the catcher's position. *Just one more, Blue, just one more,* Thomas thought to himself.

The pitch came and Chester swung with all his might. He was trying for a home run.

"Strike one," Thomas called as the bat swung through empty air.

Chester frowned and gripped the bat tighter.

"Strike two!" Thomas shouted gleefully as Chester missed again.

Chester looked at his team standing and watching silently. He looked at Thomas' team doing the same. He looked at Blue standing in the middle of the field with his tongue hanging out and his tail wagging as he waited patiently for the ball.

"Stupid dog," Chester mumbled. He gripped the bat tighter.

The next pitch came exactly where Chester wanted it. His hands tightened around the bat, his face formed into a knot, and his arms tensed. Then he swung as hard as he could and the ball went sailing high into the air.

"Yeah, Chester!" his teammates called as Chester ran to first. The other men on the bases started running as well. "Go, go, go," the team was chanting.

"Blue!" Thomas yelled.

Everyone watched as the ball sailed high over Blue's head. At first they thought he would not even chase it, but then he turned and raced for the ball. The limp seemed to disappear as Blue ran faster and faster. Fortunately, Chester hit the ball so hard and so high that Blue still had a chance.

"Go, Blue, go!" everyone but Thomas cheered. He was too nervous to cheer. If they lost, everyone would blame him and all of them would lose a lot of money.

The ball kept going for a few seconds as if it would never stop. Then as it headed towards the grass, Blue's streaking form came up from behind and he jumped in the air and caught it cleanly.

"Yee-hah! Yay! Alright!" Thomas and his teammates began to celebrate. "That a way, Blue!"

Thomas ran onto the field and tackled Blue as he ran back.

"That a way, Blue," Thomas cried, rolling in the grass, patting his fur, and scratching his head. "I knew you could do it!"

"That's one great dog you have!" Chris said as he joined Thomas and Blue in the field.

"We have," Mark corrected him. "This dog is one of us now!"

CHAPTER SEVEN

BALL'S BLUFF

After training and drilling for months, the orders finally came for the California Regiment to move out. It wasn't supposed to be a major battle, just a show of strength at a small Confederate camp across the Potomac River in Maryland. They might not even fire a shot—at least that is what the regiment had been told.

The morning of October 21, 1861, Thomas woke sometime around four in the morning, ate a quick breakfast of coffee and hardtack, and began the march. It was a raw, chilly morning that seemed to dampen Thomas' clothes as well as his spirits. Sitting and waiting for the boats to cross the Potomac River and then again on the other side for the rest of the men to finish crossing added to Thomas' dark mood. By the time everyone had gotten ashore, Thomas was miserable. To make matters worse, their commander, Colonel Baker, instructed the regiment to climb the steep, rock-infested cliff in front of them. Thomas scratched his hands twice, fell 3 times, and swore constantly as he grabbed onto random bushes and trees. He skidded sideways and backwards and, more than once, slipped back down to the bottom.

This is Ball's Bluff? Thomas thought to himself when he finally made it to the top. It was nothing spectacular. In front of him was a small field surrounded by trees, and behind him was the cliff which dropped down to the Potomac River. Someone had said that the town of Leesburg was not far beyond the trees, and the colonel had set out a small skirmishing party to scout ahead. Meanwhile, Thomas and the others formed into lines in case the Confederates should charge. When everyone had finally finished the climb there must have been over 1,500 men crowded into that little field.

A short time later gunshots and yells could be heard. Two companies of men[1] had been rushed in to help. Without even realizing what he was doing, Thomas breathed a sigh of relief when his company was chosen to stay and wait. The battle seemed fierce at times and the more he listened to the screams and the gunshots the more nervous he became. His hands grew sweaty while he gripped his rifle.

"Nervous?" Mark asked Thomas when he turned and noticed that Thomas' face had turned pale.

"A-a little," Thomas replied. Although he should have said a lot.

"Me too," Mark admitted. "I never been in any kind of fight before."

"Not even a fistfight?" Thomas asked.

"Well, maybe one or two," Mark answered.

"You seem pretty good with your gun," Thomas said, trying to reassure Mark.

"I used to hunt a lot," Mark told him. "Squirrels, rabbits, little things like that."

---

1. There are approximately 100 men in a company and 10 companies form a regiment.

"Not me," Thomas said. "I grew up in Boston. Not much hunting there."

"I thought you said you lived on a farm near Philly," Mark said in confusion.

"Oh, I do," Thomas explained. "But I grew up in Boston and then moved to the farm with my uncle and cousins last year."

Suddenly, the screams and yells from the forest grew louder and closer. Thomas and Mark turned to their left and saw the soldiers running back towards them.

"What's going on?" Thomas said anxiously.

"I don't know?" Mark replied with as much nervousness in his voice as Thomas.

"They've been beaten back," said Chris, who had been standing nearby.

"By whom?" Mark asked.

"Rebels, of course," Chris answered.

"I know it was rebels," Mark shot back. "Which unit?"

"Who knows?" Chris shrugged. "Who cares?"

No one really answered. They were too busy watching their fellow soldiers stagger back to the field. It appeared that Chris was right, the two companies of men had been pushed back and several of their officers were killed. All grew silent while they waited for the rebels to come out of the woods.

The silence was eerie. As the gunfire stopped, the screams for help grew dim and the only constant sound was the faint rhythm of a drum and bugle band playing somewhere off in the distance.

Thomas scratched the top of Blue's head, looked around the field, and wondered what would happen next. It was his first time in battle and he worried that he would not have the courage to fight. After all, the only real battle that the Union army had fought so far had been a total disaster. Thomas' regiment was not even there, but he had heard how at Bull Run, the Federal soldiers had run with their tails between their legs as the Confederate soldiers chased them almost all the way to Washington, D.C. Now, 4 months later, Thomas wondered whether things would be any different.

There were reasons to think that this time it would be better. President Lincoln had chosen a new general to take command of the army with the intention of getting it ready to fight. His name was General McClellan and he was an experienced officer of the Mexican War. So far, he had done a marvelous job of organizing the new recruits into an army. Of course, this meant that there had been very little fighting all summer and into the fall.

Thomas bent down and rubbed Blue's neck. He was so glad the dog was at his side. As their company's mascot, Blue had been allowed to go everywhere with the men, including the battles. Many officers realized that mascots had a calming influence on soldiers, sometimes providing distractions or entertainment and occasionally inspiring the men. Thomas appreciated Blue a little more today as he gently rubbed his fur, trying to forget about the battle that would soon be upon him.

Some gunfire could still be heard in the woods. More than a thousand men were standing on the bluff yet every one of them was quiet, waiting for something to happen. No birds sang, no crickets chirped. It was spooky. Thomas began to fidget. As he looked around, a chill traveled up his spine.

Blue's head suddenly shot up and his tail stopped wagging. Mark noticed the sudden change in the dog.

"They're coming!" he shouted.

Suddenly bullets flew through the air, musket fire boomed in Thomas' ears, and smoke puffed into the sky. The Confederates were attacking.

"Fire!" several officers shouted.

Thomas lifted up his gun and fired. He winced in pain as the explosions from hundreds of his fellow soldiers' guns almost burst his eardrums. He staggered back a little as the recoil from his gun pushed it against his shoulder. Mark grabbed Thomas with his right hand and steadied him.

"Reload!" the order came.

Bullets were flying everywhere. Men were screaming, guns were roaring, grass and dirt fell on the men as the battle grew more fierce. Amidst it all, Blue was running in circles, barking and chasing bullets left and right.

A bullet hit Mark in the shoulder. He screamed, staggered back, and fell.

"Mark!" Thomas screamed as he bent down to help his friend.

"Don't worry about me," Mark cried, placing his hand over his bloody shoulder. "Keep fighting."

Thomas looked around. There wasn't anyone to help Mark right now. The men were all busy trying to repel the Confederates, who kept coming.

"Blue!" Thomas exclaimed as he saw the dog approach. "Good dog."

Blue put his nose down on Mark's head and rubbed him gently. Mark reached up and began to pet the dog. "Good boy," he said.

Thomas stood up and smiled. The dog would keep Mark calm for the minute. Then his stomach felt as if it had dropped to his knees as he looked around and saw the chaos around him. Men were running, shooting, falling, and dying. Explosions from the guns of both armies became constant. Smoke from the rifles spread through the air making it difficult to see. Thomas thought he saw a U.S. flag, then a Confederate flag. Some men were fighting hand-to-hand. Thomas froze. He didn't know what to do.

"Fire, you idiot, fire!" someone yelled at him. It was Chester. "They're pushing us back!"

All of the drilling paid off as Thomas lifted his gun and, without even thinking, pulled the trigger. He didn't know if he hit anyone but at least he had done something.

"The colonel is down!" Thomas heard someone shout after the fighting had grown even more intense. "What do we do? What do we do?"

Thomas looked ahead. The enemy was getting much closer. There was still a U.S. flag flying in front of him but even that was destroyed after a few minutes. Men were falling all around Thomas and he was beginning to panic.

A sword whisked through the air and cut the top of his hat in two. Thomas turned and saw a man in grey about to take another swing. Thomas jumped back.

"Nooo!" Thomas screamed as the man with the sword came closer. "Don't!"

The man lifted his sword and was about to swing when out of nowhere a figure jumped through the air and smashed the man to the ground.

"Blue!" Thomas yelled.

The man on the ground was stunned for a moment, with Blue standing on his chest. Then he swore and swung his sword at Blue.

"Nooo!" Thomas screamed again as he saw the sword slice off a piece of Blue's fur.

Blue barked in surprise and fell back, shocked by the sudden cut. The man started to get up. Thomas screamed, grabbed his rifle, and stabbed the man in the chest with his bayonet.

"Aaarggh," the man moaned, grabbing Thomas' rifle with both his hands before he died.

Thomas pulled out the bayonet, staggered backwards and looked down. It was the first time he had killed a man with his bare hands. He couldn't believe what he had done. All of that talk about war, fighting, shooting, and killing didn't make any difference. Nothing could prepare Thomas for the shadow of death and the guilt that came with realizing he had just murdered somebody. On the dirt, with blood flowing from his chest and a look of unbearable pain on his face, laid the man that Thomas had just killed. He seemed to be staring straight at Thomas. Thomas didn't know what to say. He just froze up again.

"Look out!" Thomas heard Mark shout from his position on the ground. He was still lying there, waiting for help as the fight continued around him. "Thomas, they're all around you!"

The Confederates were everywhere. One moment he had been standing amongst his own comrades, shooting at the enemy across the field, and the next he was surrounded. Bullets scratched his skin and pierced holes in his uniform. Enemy soldiers charged with their bayonets at the Union soldiers who turned tail and ran.

Thomas turned and ran as fast as he could, like everyone else. They headed back towards the bluff and the river below.

"Thomas!" he heard Mark cry. "Help me!"

Thomas turned to see Mark being overrun by Confederate soldiers. Blue had tried to drag Mark in the dirt, but some rebel soldier had knocked Blue with his rifle and chased him off. The Confederates surrounded Mark and made him a prisoner.

"Mark!" Thomas cried, but it was too late. The Confederates had taken Mark prisoner and they would soon reach Thomas if he didn't hustle.

Thomas turned and ran as fast as he could. The bullets singed his skin and swiped past his ears. His fellow soldiers fell all around him, pushing and shoving while trying to make their way to the cliff. Thomas jumped over one man, fell, and started to roll down the cliff. As he stumbled out of control, men leaped over him into the water or onto the rocks or landed on their fellow soldiers. It was the scariest thing Thomas had ever experienced.

He reached the bottom of the cliff and staggered up. His bones were bruised, his muscles ached, he was bleeding in five places, but he could still move. The screams grew louder. He heard splashing and yelling as the men jumped in the water to try to escape the deadly bullets that still flew in their direction.

Thomas jumped into the water. He swam in any direction to get away from the bluff. He had trouble controlling his movements. There were hundreds of men

in the water banging about and trying to avoid the bullets. The water was deep and flowing so rapidly that
Thomas struggled to stay afloat. He gagged and spit out
water. He flailed around trying to get clear of the men
around him. Someone who had trouble swimming
grabbed onto Thomas and started pulling at him.

"Let go! Let go!" Thomas screamed at the man.
"You're dragging me down!"

The man in a complete panic hacked and coughed
and grabbed at Thomas trying to stay afloat. Thomas
tried to swim away, but the man's weight was pulling
him down.

"Let go!" Thomas screamed as his head went under water.

Thomas violently swung his arms trying to free
the man. He felt he would explode from the inside as
his lungs filled up with water. He punched, jabbed, and
kicked but the man was still hanging on. Finally, just
as Thomas felt his eyes start to close, the man's arms
grew limp and his grip loosened. Thomas kicked violently upwards and pushed his head into the air.

"Haaaaaaahhhh!" he cried as his lungs took in the
sweet, wonderful air. "Haaaahhhhh," he breathed again.

Thomas looked around. The water was flowing fast,
men were panicking and jumping in everywhere. The
bullets were still piercing the water and killing men.
Thomas moved his arms trying to get away but he was
too tired from the battle with the other soldier. He took
another deep breath and his head went under one final time. Then, everything went dark.

Chapter Eight

Running

"Huck, huck, ahh-huck," Thomas coughed, spat, and hacked out all of the water in his lungs. He lifted his head and opened his eyes. The fighting was over, the soldiers were gone, and Thomas was alone in the middle of the night on the shore of the Potomac River.

A wet tongue licked his face. Startled, Thomas turned and saw Blue standing over him, his tail wagging and his tongue drooping out of his jaw and off to the side.

"Blue!" Thomas exclaimed. "You're alright!"

Thomas rose, wrapped his arms around the dog, and gave him a big hug. "You're a good dog, Blue," Thomas continued, leaning back a little so he could scratch the top of Blue's head. "You're a good dog."

A gunshot rang somewhere in the distance. Both Thomas and Blue lifted their heads and turned in the direction of the sound. Through the darkness, Thomas could hear noises of men moving with shouts of anger and concern.

"They must be looking for us," Thomas said to Blue. "The battle is over and now they're looking for all the wounded and dead."

Thomas shuddered as he remembered the fight on the bluff. His chest heaved as the pain of drowning returned with the memories.

"I ain't going back," he said suddenly, with determination. "I'm not entering that craziness again. Not for all the money in the world."

Thomas stood and looked around to determine where the sounds were coming from. "C'mon, Blue," he said as he turned and ran in the opposite direction, "let's get out of here."

Thomas ran as far away from the fighting as he could. And as he ran, images of the fighting and of drowning kept flickering in and out of his mind. *This was supposed to be an adventure,* Thomas thought to himself as he ran. *This was supposed to be fun. It wasn't supposed to be like that. We were supposed to win. We weren't supposed to kill each other, jumping all over ourselves and struggling to even survive. That's not what it was supposed to be.*

He ran through the woods and the fields. No matter how hard he ran, he couldn't stop thinking about the bluff. The image of Mark being dragged away tormented him, making him jump at every strange sound and sight. Finally, when he could run no more, he sat down on the grass, put his head on Blue's soft belly, and promptly fell asleep.

The next day Thomas awoke in pain; he looked at his left arm and saw that he had been shot. In all of the confusion yesterday he hadn't even noticed. Now, he couldn't help but wince at the constant stinging in his arm. Fortunately, it was not a very deep wound although it would be enough to leave a scar. He looked around for something to wipe off the blood. During the chaos of yesterday's battle, he had lost his haversack, canteen, cartridge box containing his gunpowder, and even his rifle! He was in the middle of nowhere with no food, no weapon, and no idea what to do.

Thomas tore off a piece of his shirt near the waist and wrapped it around his injured arm. "That ought to do it," he said, sitting up and placing his back against the tree. "Now it's time to figure out what to do."

Thomas casually patted Blue's back as he considered his options. There was no way he was going back; he didn't care if it was considered desertion. It was too crazy and scary for him. Being made fun of and feeling bored back at the farm was much better than getting shot at. Besides, he was looking forward to seeing Mary. But what would he tell her? She was sure to call him a coward, unless he showed her his arm and made it seem worse than it was. That was a good idea. If he was wounded, no one would wonder why he was home and after the disaster at the bluff, the regiment would just think he was lost. Thomas smiled as the plan began to form in his head. "Now all I have to do is figure out a way to get home," he said out loud.

Getting home turned out to be easier than he thought. There were enough soldiers who were wounded or on leave that no one asked him any questions. If anything, people were more helpful to him once they saw that he was a soldier. One woman offered him a piece of pie, another a whole meal, and one family even offered to let him spend the night.

It was a long walk, of course. Over one hundred miles separated Maryland from his home in Pennsylvania. Fortunately, Thomas was used to walking and marching.

Having Blue with him made it much easier. The dog was a great companion. He always did what Thomas told him to do, he never complained, and he made a great pillow. If Thomas could not scrape up food enough to share with Blue, the dog would wander off and find his own.

By the time they reached Thomas' home in Farmington it was November. The nights were beginning to get very cold and Thomas had started to make fires after sunset to keep Blue and himself warm. His arm was much worse and he didn't think he'd have to fake anything with Mary. It really did look awful. Although the bleeding had stopped, it had turned dark black and he was having trouble even moving it. *Maybe Mary can do something with it,* Thomas thought to himself as he approached the farm. *She always was good at fixing people up.*

The town didn't look much different from the last time he saw it. There were less people out and about and everyone who was out appeared busy. The biggest change was the foliage. When Thomas left in the summer, everything had been in full bloom, the grass and leaves were a bright green, and the cornstalks stood over his head. Now all of the leaves had begun to change color and fall to the ground. Autumn was Thomas' favorite time of year. He loved all of the pretty reds, greens, yellows, oranges, and pinks that painted the sky. He especially loved jumping into the huge piles of leaves after a long day of raking.

No one was raking outdoors today though. A slight drizzle was in the air and the day was overcast and dark, which made the leaves too heavy to rake. It also gave everyone a good excuse to huddle inside next to the fire and sip on some warm soup. As Thomas looked at the chimney on top of his house, he could see that there was indeed a fire inside, and he smacked his lips thinking of the warm meal that awaited him.

Thomas nervously knocked on the door. He heard a chair move and soft footsteps approach. The handle made a "click" as it turned and the door opened slowly.

"Hello?" Mary said softly.

"Hi, Mary," Thomas said with a smile.

"Thomas!" Mary screamed as she jumped into his arms. "Thomas!"

"Thomas?" Aunt Patricia said from inside the room. She turned her head and looked towards the open door. "My Lord! What is he doing here?"

"We thought you were dead!" Mary screamed into his ear as she hugged him again.

"Dad wrote and said you were lost!" Thomas' cousin Rachel cried as she too stood up and ran to the door.

"Well obviously he's been found," Rachel's sister Jamie said smartly.

"But what are you doing here?" Aunt Patricia said coldly. There was a hint of suspicion in her voice that worried Thomas.

"What does it matter?" Mary asked enthusiastically. She jumped at Thomas and hugged him one more time. "He's alive!"

"Ouch!" Thomas yelled as Mary squeezed his sore arm.

Mary jumped back. "Thomas, you're wounded," she gasped. "What happened? Are you alright? Come in, let me look at you."

"It's nothing," Thomas boasted as he walked inside the house. He was relieved that Aunt Patricia's question had been forgotten for the moment.

"Ruff, ruff!" Alfie suddenly barked in his high-pitched voice.

"Alfie!" Thomas cried. He bent down and held out his arms. "Come here, boy!"

Alfie ran toward Thomas and jumped into his waiting arms. Thomas hugged him tightly, but he couldn't help notice that the dog's leg was lame and he ran with a clear limp.

"Roff, roff!" Blue suddenly barked in a deep bark.

Alfie jumped back but did not run away. "Ruff, ruff, ruff," he yelled back at the big canine.

"Don't worry about him, boy," Thomas said to Alfie, rubbing Blue's head and bringing him close. "He's a friend."

"Wow!" Helen shouted. It was the first time Thomas had noticed her. He couldn't believe how she had grown in the short time he had been gone. She didn't look so much like a baby anymore and she had to be at least up to his belly in height now. "Where did you get him?"

"I found him a couple of months ago," Thomas explained. "He's been a great friend to everyone and he even saved my life!"

"Saved your life?" Aunt Patricia repeated.

"Well, I think he did," Thomas said awkwardly. He continued to pet both Alfie and Blue while the two dogs looked jealously at each other. "I had fallen into this river during that terrible battle and another soldier had panicked and pulled me down. I managed to get away from him but I was so tired that I couldn't swim anymore. The next thing I know, I am waking up on the shore of the Potomac with Blue standing over me."

"Wow!" Jamie said. "That dog is a hero!"

"No, he's not," Rachel said doubtfully. "Thomas doesn't even remember what happened. He's just imagining the dog saved him."

"I am not!" Thomas yelled back.

"Thomas," Aunt Patricia interrupted before a fight could begin. She was losing her patience and wanted to get an answer to her original question. "Why are you here?"

"He's wounded, Auntie," Mary answered for Thomas.

"Not that badly," Aunt Patricia said coldly. "And where's the dressing. That wound looks like it was never looked at."

Thomas and Mary stared at his arm.

"Thomas," Aunt Patricia said sternly, "did they look at it and send you home?"

All eyes turned to Thomas. He looked down at the ground without an immediate answer.

"Thomas?" Aunt Patricia repeated.

"No," Thomas mumbled. "No one looked at it."

Everyone stood quietly, waiting for Thomas to continue. He looked at his aunt and Mary. They both looked upset.

"Why not?" Aunt Patricia asked finally when it was clear that Thomas was not going to speak.

"I didn't go back to camp," Thomas said shamefully. He felt guilty as the truth of what he had done finally hit him. "I was too afraid. They had left me for dead: all alone on the shores of the river in the middle of the night. I guess I panicked and ran."

"You ran?" Mary said softly. She knew her brother was not the most courageous boy. After all, Mary had saved Thomas more than once when he ran from the local bullies. But she couldn't believe that he ran away from his unit, his responsibility.

"I didn't mean to," Thomas said. "I just did it. My legs started to move and I couldn't stop. I ran and ran and by the time I had calmed down I had run so far that I just kept going."

"How could you do that?" Rachel scolded. "How could you quit and leave your regiment behind? Don't you have any sense of responsibility?"

"You don't know what it was like!" Thomas shouted. His voice was beginning to crack as he struggled to hold back the tears. "It wasn't just the bullets or the men dying all around me. It was everything. Have you ever almost drowned? Do you know what it's like to have your lungs so full of water that you keep sinking and feel like your chest is going to explode?"

No one said anything. Helen held tightly onto the little doll that she had been holding.

"And it was one of my own regiment who was drowning me," Thomas went on. "It was the worst experience I ever had in my life. I almost died."

"That's war, young man," Aunt Patricia said. There was no compassion in her voice and her eyes were cold and unfeeling. "That's what you signed up for. I tried to tell you that you were too young, but you had to be the smart little boy and run off just like your brother, David, did."

Thomas did not look up. He hated when Aunt Patricia lectured him.

"Well, now you know what it's like," Aunt Patricia continued. "And you've brought shame and dishonor to our entire family."

"Oh, Aunt Patricia," Mary spoke up, "it's not that horrible. Thomas is just a boy. How can he dishonor the entire family?"

"Don't argue with me, young lady," Aunt Patricia replied. "I'm in no mood for one of your tirades. Thomas has disgraced this family and he will continue to disgrace this family until he grows up and finds a way to make up for what he's done."

Aunt Patricia stormed out of the room, followed by her daughters. Mary looked down at Thomas sitting next to his two dogs. "So much for my homecoming," Thomas mumbled.

Chapter Nine

Badge of Shame

Strangely enough, Aunt Patricia was against Thomas returning to his unit. Since he had started this whole thing by disobeying his uncle in the first place, she believed it was just as well that he stay home now. He had already dishonored the family once by running and she didn't want him to do it again. In addition, she needed his help around the house since all of the other boys were gone.

The only problem would be what to tell the neighbors and Uncle Robert. She couldn't let him continue to think that Thomas was dead, and the neighbors would want to know what Thomas was doing home for so long. Soldiers earned leave to visit family, especially around the Christmas holidays, but leave would never last as long as Thomas was planning to stay. So, she decided to use Thomas' wound as her excuse to keep him there. Mary had treated it so that it would heal alright, but he would have to wear the bandages for as long as the war lasted to hide the truth. It would be a badge of shame, a constant reminder to him of what he had done, she said to Thomas.

70

Wearing the bandages gained him some respect from Joey, Peter, and Bobby. They looked at him as almost a war hero, at least for a little while. They stopped being so mean and even talked to Thomas as if he was one of the gang.

Blue and Alfie got along great. Thomas was afraid that Alfie would be jealous or that Blue would not want to play with a small, lame dog, but the two became fast friends. They would wrestle, run, bark, and jump and even though Blue was better at every thing they did, he would take it easy on Alfie and even let him win sometimes.

Thomas could enjoy none of this. He couldn't help feeling guilty about what he had done. Every time he walked into the house, his family treated him like a criminal. They barely talked to him (except to order him around), stared coldly at him, and sometimes talked about him at the table as if he wasn't even there. Only Mary and Helen treated him alright. They had been angry and embarrassed as well by what he had done, but they couldn't stay angry at him the way the others could.

He had no free time at all. Aunt Patricia made him do chores constantly and he never could finish what she wanted done. Because of his bandages he could never use his left arm completely. Even raking leaves took hours. *Now I know why I ran off to join the army,* Thomas would say to himself.

The months went by and winter turned into spring and spring into summer. The war grew worse for the United States, and also for Thomas. With each new disaster for the Union army, Thomas continued to feel guilty. Even worse, Joey, Peter, and Bobby began to lose respect for the army and, therefore, for Thomas. They began to pick on him again. This time, it was for being part of a losing army instead of the insults from before Thomas left for the war.

"Your old General McClellan don't know how to fight," Peter accused Thomas one day as they met while walking down the road. "Every time he has a chance to do something important he waits for General Lee to beat him up again."

"That ain't so," Thomas said half-heartedly. He wasn't sure if he believed in McClellan anymore either. It seemed that he never did anything except wait for reinforcements.

"Sure it is," Bobby added. "He was so close to Richmond that they could smell 'em."

"Yeah," agreed Peter. "But instead of attacking, he waited so long that Lee got the chance to beat him again and he had to go running home."

"That's cuz General Jackson was threatening the capital!" Thomas said defensively.

"With less men," Bobby replied disdainfully. "Them rebs seem to keep beating you guys with less men and less resources. It's no wonder my pa won't let me fight."

"You never said your pa won't let you fight," Thomas said quickly, trying to turn the argument in his favor. "You said it was cuz he needed you on the farm."

"Uh, it is," Bobby answered slowly. "That's why he won't let me fight."

"He won't let you?" Thomas asked. "Or you don't want to?"

"Want to?" Bobby asked in shock. "Why would I want to? Your army is led by a bunch of dolts who can't seem to do anything right. All you ever do is waste time and waste lives."

Thomas didn't answer. All he could think was what he had heard about the Battle of Shiloh: the bloodiest battle in American history. With 13,000 men killed, wounded, or missing for the Union, and 10,000 for the Confederacy, Shiloh had the terrible reputation of killing more Americans in two days than in all other wars before it combined.

"This war is a joke," Joey said, taking over for Bobby. "It all started because Lincoln wouldn't let the Southerners do what they wanted and then you idiots run off and join up just cuz he asks us."

"We joined to defend our country!" Thomas yelled in an angry tone. It was one thing to criticize the way the war was fought, but it was a completely different story to make fun of those who had risked their lives to enlist.

"What country?" Joey replied. "The United States of America? We ain't United anymore. We are the conquering states of America. We march down South and tell them people that they have to be part of our country when they don't want to."

"They can't just leave," Thomas argued.

"Why not?" Joey shot back. "They joined on their own. Why can't they leave on their own?"

"Because they can't," Thomas answered quickly. He could think of nothing else to say. It had always seemed so obvious to him. *How could a state just quit the United States of America once it had joined? It couldn't. The country would just fall apart.*

"Oh, good answer," Peter interrupted. "You learn that one in the school you went to?"

"Shut up, Peter," Thomas said boldly. His face had turned red with anger and his arms had begun to shake. For years now kids had been ridiculing and teasing him. He had never been able to fight back because there was always more of them and they were all bigger. Now, however, things had changed. Thomas was almost as tall as them, had experienced war, and had felt what it was like to have people trying to kill him. Compared to that, Bobby, Peter, and Joey didn't look so threatening anymore.

"Make me," Peter challenged.

Thomas swung his fist hard and fast. The sudden move caught Peter off guard allowing Thomas to hit him squarely in the nose. Blood started to pour down Peter's cheeks.

"You little...," Peter cussed as he lunged at Thomas.

"Get him, Pete!" Joey and Bobby yelled.

Thomas dodged out of the way and Peter went stumbling into the dirt.

"I learned a few things in the army," Thomas grinned. Peter stood up and rushed again.

"Raarrr!" Peter cried.

Thomas dodged again. This time, Peter was able to catch Thomas' foot and knock him off balance. He jumped on top of Thomas and began punching him in the stomach. Each blow knocked the breath out of Thomas just like when he had almost drowned. The two boys continued to roll on the dirt together, trading blows and yelling at each other.

"Get him, Peter, get him!" Joey and Bobby chanted.

Thomas managed to wriggle free and stood up panting.

"Had enough?" he challenged Peter. Finally, Thomas was able to hold his own against these guys. *At least the army had been good for something,* Thomas thought.

"No way," Peter answered. He held his fists in front of his face, but his legs were shaky and he stumbled a bit.

Thomas swung hard: a left and a right and another left. Peter's head fell back with each blow and then he fell to the ground, bruised and bleeding. Thomas proudly stood over him smiling.

"Hey," Joey said suddenly, pointing to the torn arm brace that Thomas had been wearing. "Your arm is fine!"

"He ain't wounded!" Bobby shouted.

Thomas looked down at his arm. It was perfectly healthy. The only thing left of his brace was a few rags hanging from his elbow. His stomach sank as he realized his secret had been revealed.

"You lied!" Peter said, wiping the blood off his face and starting to sit up. "You ain't never been wounded."

Thomas started to back up, shaking his head back and forth, unable to say a word.

"You liar!" Bobby yelled.

"Liar!" Peter and Joey joined in.

Thomas turned and ran. Everybody would know the secret and nothing would ever be the same again.

CHAPTER TEN

NOWHERE TO RUN

Thomas didn't dare leave the house. Everyone in the entire town now knew that he had deserted from the army and had pretended about his being wounded. His deception angered some people; others joked about his cowardice. A few of the town leaders called for his arrest as a deserter. The only thing that prevented them from taking any action was his young age. Punishing a boy didn't seem right.

Even Aunt Patricia pretended that Thomas had fooled her. She realized the seriousness of his trouble and she didn't want the family to suffer because of it. Desertion was a serious crime and soldiers who deserted could be imprisoned or even shot! At every opportunity, she reminded the townspeople and Thomas that he was not her son, only her nephew. Her real sons, Aunt Patricia would say over and over again, were still fighting bravely for the Union.

Mary was angry at him, too. Not because he had fooled the townspeople but because of how he was hiding in the house. "Every time you have a problem," she had scolded Thomas, "you run away from it. You ran from Joey, Peter, and Bobby when they teased you. You

76

ran away to join the army when you didn't like farm life. You ran from the army when things got bad and now you run from everyone and hide in the house. When are you going to grow up?"

Thomas had no response for Mary. She was right. He had always run from his troubles. But he didn't know what else to do. Ever since his parents died and his brother David disappeared, he had been all alone. He had no one to help him, no one to give him advice except Mary, who was now angry at him.

Thomas' dogs could not even escape his problems. The anger and disgust that people felt towards Thomas were also directed at his dogs. No one would play with them, pat them, or even feed them. Aunt Patricia had threatened to send Alfie away since it was obvious his leg would never heal properly.

To make things worse, the war continued to go badly for the Union. The Federals had more men than the Confederates, more factories, more railroads, and a navy that blockaded the entire Southern coast; yet, the inept Union generals kept losing more and more men. President Lincoln had to ask the country for more volunteers again and by August the government had requested over half a million men. Thomas' guilt was overwhelming him.

"Here's something that won't make you feel any better," Mary said bitterly one day as she tossed an envelope onto the table. "It looks like a letter from one of your buddies in the regiment."

Thomas lifted his head and looked at the letter addressed to him. The address, unclear and messy, had been written in a hurry or by a weak hand.

"Where'd you get this?" Thomas asked Mary, who was still standing over him.

"It was in a letter sent by Uncle Robert. He said it was sent to the regiment a short time ago and he forwarded it to you."

"Oh," Thomas said sadly. The letter was obviously written by someone who still thought he was in the army. This letter would not be fun to read.

"Aren't you going to open it?" Mary urged him.

"Yeah, I guess so," Thomas said slowly as he lifted the envelope again and opened it.

"Whoa!" Thomas whistled out loud as he unfolded the letter. "It's from Mark."

"Mark?" Mary repeated. "Who's Mark?"

"He was my best friend in the regiment," Thomas answered quickly as his eyes scanned the paper. "He was captured at Ball's Bluff and now he says he's in a prison in Richmond!"

"My Lord," Mary cried. "What's he say?"

"Well, most of it is questions about me and Blue," Thomas explained. "He was pretty fond of the dog and he wants to know if he made it out O.K."

"Does he describe the prison at all?" Mary wondered. She knew that the two armies were working on some kind of prisoner exchange program for all the soldiers who had been captured. With the battles increasing in number the prisoners of war grew beyond anyone's expectations. She heard the conditions were terrible in the prisons.

"Not much," Thomas answered simply. "It seems like he doesn't want to talk about it. He talks a little about how crowded it is and how little food he gets. Then he describes the poor health of many of the men.

He says that he was lucky enough not to be badly wounded and he should be alright for now. The men who were wounded are getting very little care and are getting much worse. He said he's seen 10 men die in the last 2 weeks."

"Oh my," Mary said softly, covering her mouth with her hands. "This war is so terrible, so terrible. Men killing each other, boys fighting, starvation and sickness in the prisons and in the camps. I don't understand how we can do this to each other."

Thomas did not respond. He still held the letter in his hand and was rereading it. The words swirled in and out of his head as the Battle of Ball's Bluff and Thomas' run from it replayed in his mind. *What would Mark say if he knew that Thomas was safe and sound at home?*

Mary looked at Thomas' slumped shoulders and bent head. In all of her anger at Thomas she had forgotten the terrible things that had happened to him in the army. She had been so mean and cruel to him without ever once thinking about what he must be going through. *Poor Thomas*, she thought to herself as she gently put her hand on his shoulder to comfort him. All of her anger and bitterness slowly disappeared from her as she finally recognized the anguish in Thomas' head and heart.

He must feel so ashamed, so guilty, Mary thought to herself. *I don't know how he can bear it.* She felt embarassed that she had not been more understanding. Her stomach tightened and her throat became dry.

"Thomas," she said quietly, "I think it's time for you to see something."

Thomas looked up quietly at his sister. His face was soft and his eyes were swelling with water. Mary felt another stab of guilt and turned quickly towards her bedroom.

"I'll be right back," she reassured him.

Thomas looked down and began to scratch Blue's head. He felt no curiosity or wonder at what Mary was doing. He was too drained and tired for that. Everything that he had gone through had just attacked his memories and his feelings. He felt weak and exhausted, as if he had lost the game of life and was ready to surrender.

Mary hurried back into the room. "Here," she said as she handed a folded up piece of paper to Thomas. "It's from David."

"David?" Thomas said with a hint of excitement. The energy was starting to come back into his body as he thought of his brother.

"Yes David," Mary answered with enthusiasm. She knew that this would lift Thomas out of his mood. He had always loved and admired his older brother. David had taken Thomas with him everywhere he went, he had taught him how to fight, and how to throw a baseball. Then, when David disappeared 2 years ago to look for their Dad, it was as if they had lost their father all over again. Mary had cried herself to sleep many nights and little Helen had stopped talking for a whole week.

"He wrote us about a month ago," Mary explained, "but I didn't want to show you until you were ready for it."

"Ready for it?" Thomas repeated in confusion and anger. "What do you mean ready for it?"

"It's pretty serious," Mary replied. "He's in Georgia trying to free his slave friend Lisa and he says some stuff I'm not sure you're ready to hear."

"What do you mean?" Thomas asked a little nervously.

"Just read it," Mary prompted as she sat next to him.

Thomas slowly began to read the letter which started with an apology for his disappearance and for not writing sooner. He further explained that he had located his friend Lisa, a slave on a plantation outside of Savannah, and had planned to rescue her and take her to a nearby Union base. Skimming over the details, Thomas continued to read David's words that strangely began to sound more like their Dad's preachings about the war.

"This doesn't sound like David," Thomas said to Mary, looking up from the letter. "Why did you want me to read it?"

"Did you get to the part where he talks directly to you?" Mary asked quietly.

"No," Thomas said slowly.

"Read it," Mary commanded.

Thomas, the letter began. *I'm sorry I can't discuss this in person but I don't have much choice. I'm doing something very important here. I'm trying to save a life, to set free another human being. I'm sorry I'm not there anymore to play ball with you or beat up on Joshua, but times have changed. I've changed. I'm not the David you remember.*

"This is weird," Thomas interrupted himself again.

"I know," Mary agreed. "But keep reading. It's important."

I was with Mom just before she died. She made me realize that even though Dad was a little crazy at times the cause that he fought for was the most holy cause since God set the Jews free from Egypt.

You always knew that Mom and Dad were abolitionists. You knew that they worked to try to free the slaves before the war began. You probably even know that they were involved with the John Brown raid. But I don't know if you realize how important their work was. Slavery is a dark, despicable evil that stains our nation and insults our Lord. How can people own other people? We are all equal in the eyes of the Lord, but these slave masters make their slaves do whatever they want! You know this, Thomas. You've read about it in school. You've heard Mom and Dad talk about it, practically every night. You were with me when we talked to Lisa. I know you understand what I am talking about.

But this war is in danger. The North is losing. Even worse, they are not even fighting to end slavery. I'm sure you've heard Lincoln say that this war is about the Union and not slavery. He still refuses to free any slaves or to let black people fight on our side! If nothing is done soon, the slaves will be in chains forever!

You've got to do something. You've got to get involved. I know you're still young but we can't let that stop us. Mom and Dad died working to free the slaves and we can't let their deaths mean nothing. If you could join up and fight, then that would mean so much to their memory. Maybe you can convince your fellow soldiers to change their attitudes about the war: get them to realize that this must be a fight to end slavery instead of just some battle between states over government and constitution.

I know you're scared, Thomas. But I also know that you are one of the bravest boys I ever knew. You were always there with me when we fought bigger boys trying to bully us. You never ran and you always wanted to be with me and my friends.

Thomas, you look more like Dad than I ever did. You have Mom's fire and spirit in you. You need to honor that, Thomas. You need to realize who you are and where you come from. I know that you'll do it. I know that you will see that Mom and Dad's dream doesn't die. Good luck, brother. I'll see you when you march down. Give Helen a kiss for me.

Love,
David

Thomas hung his head in despair. Now what could he do?

Chapter Eleven

Dogs

"Thomas," Mary said softly after a few seconds. She placed her hand on his shoulder. "Are you alright?"

"Yeah, I guess...I don't know," Thomas said in a shaky voice. The letter was still in his hands and his head was bent toward the table.

"What are you going to do?" Mary wondered aloud.

"I don't know," Thomas replied.

"Are you going to return to the army?"

"I don't know," he repeated.

"What about what David said?" Mary continued.

"I don't know! I don't know! I don't know!" Thomas shouted pushing the chair onto the floor as he stood. The dogs backed away in the corner. "How many times do you want me to say that?"

"I'm sorry," Mary apologized in a soft voice. "I was just—"

"Well don't!" Thomas interrupted. "I've had enough of you and everyone else trying to tell me what to do. All of you want to make my decisions for me! First, you don't want me to sign up, then you do, and now David writes this mysterious letter trying to convince me to join him on his stupid crusade to free the slaves."

"It's not stupid and you know it!" Mary shouted. She knew that she shouldn't get angry at Thomas. He didn't mean what he said but she couldn't help herself. She felt too strongly about freeing the slaves to contain herself.

"Why should I risk my life for someone else," Thomas went on, "someone I don't even know? Huh? What did they do for me?"

Mary was about to answer him but she managed to keep quiet this time.

"What did they do for anyone? They're just stupid slaves. And you and David and everyone else think I should go run off and die for them!"

"No, Thomas, no one wants you to die."

"Well, that's what's going to happen if I go back!" Thomas, almost out of control now, was waving his hands in the air and pacing back and forth. "You don't know what it's like, you can't imagine. The enemy is trying to kill you, to put a bullet or bayonet through your heart, or blow your head off with a cannonball. And they don't stop until you are dead, or they are!"

Mary didn't respond. She had read enough about the war and had seen the wounded soldiers in the aid stations to understand what Thomas was describing to her. *Maybe it was crazy asking him to return. Maybe she should just leave him alone.*

"You can't make me go back!" Thomas shouted. "No one can! Not you, not David, not anyone!" Thomas turned and headed out the door, slamming it behind him.

"Oh, Thomas," Mary said softly as she opened the door and watched him storm away. Alfie and Blue snuck around her and through the door to be with Thomas. "I'm so sorry."

Thomas continued to walk through the grass with his two dogs at his side. He was too angry and frustrated to care where he was going even though in the back of his mind he knew that if anyone saw him it could mean trouble for him.

"Thomas, Thomas!" a small voice called to him from elsewhere in the field. "Wait! Wait!"

Thomas turned to see his little sister Helen running towards him. He had hardly spent any time at all with her since he returned from the war and as she ran towards him he noticed how much she had grown. She was no longer the tiny little girl he once knew. *She must be nine by now*, Thomas thought as he watched her run towards him. Her red hair had grown thick and long, down below her shoulders. As she ran, it swayed back and forth in the wind like a kite sailing gently on the breeze.

"Where are you going?" Helen said in between breaths once she had reached Thomas. Her bright green eyes still burned with that energy and vibrance that Thomas had always loved.

"Nowhere," Thomas answered simply. Just the sight of Helen had drained the anger from him. Whenever she was around, Thomas' face lit up and his heart beat a little lighter. As the baby of the family, she always had this effect on Thomas. Indeed, the whole family—aunts, uncles, older brother and sister, cousins, and parents loved, adored and, of course, spoiled her.

"Can I come with you?" Helen asked politely. She loved Thomas as much as he loved her. He was her big brother, her protector, and she loved how he hugged her and tucked her in at night. "I haven't spent any time with you since you came back."

"Sure," Thomas answered with a slight smile. Helen returned his smile with a big grin and a jump in the air.

"Goody!" she cried.

Thomas held her hand lightly and headed towards the big oak tree. "Let's sit here and look at the clouds," Thomas suggested once they arrived at the tree. The trunk of the old tree was so large that Thomas could only wrap his arms halfway around it. Its long branches and big green leaves created a wonderful shade over the field. Thomas and Helen had often come here to rest under its shadow and lie on the grass as they stared into the sky.

"O.K.!" Helen agreed pleasantly. "Can we try to look for dragons?"

"Sure," Thomas laughed. It was amazing how quickly he could forget his troubles. Helen just seemed to have that effect on him. Her love and charm were contagious.

Lying on their backs and staring into the sky together, Thomas felt the wind gently rolling over him as it swayed his hair back and forth. He listened to the birds singing in the trees, rubbed his hand gently along the grass, and played absent-mindedly with the soft blades. *What a beautiful day,* he thought.

"I see a dog," Helen said after a few minutes.

"Yeah, me too," Thomas agreed. "And next to it is a horse. See it?"

"I think so," Helen replied in her cute little voice. "And there's a cat and a butterfly."

"Uh-huh," Thomas said. "And way over there is a huge one. Looks like, ummm a wagon."

"I don't see a wagon," Helen responded. "But I do see a pitchfork."

"A pitchfork?" Thomas questioned doubtfully. "Where do you see a pitchfork?"

"Over there," Helen pointed, "next to the cat."

"That's not a pitchfork, that's a flag."

"A flag?" Helen repeated. "Where do you see a flag?"

"Right there," Thomas pointed up and towards his right. "See that rectangular-looking cloud."

"I don't see a flag," Helen admitted.

"Look," Thomas pointed again with a little bit of frustration in his voice. "Next to the dog and the gun."

"What gun?"

"The one with the bayonet," Thomas explained. "See? There's a gun and a flag and even a cannon wheel over there."

"Thomas, what are you talking about?" Helen wondered. "I don't see any of those things."

Thomas stopped pointing and slowly lowered his hands. He was thinking about the war again. He felt drained and depressed. He couldn't escape it. It was following him everywhere.

"What's wrong, Thomas?" Helen asked when Thomas lowered his head and rolled over on his belly putting his face in the grass. "Don't you want to look for dragons?"

"No," Thomas said. "I already have real dragons to worry about."

"Huh?" Helen said. "What do you mean?"

"Never mind," Thomas waved his hand. "You wouldn't understand."

"You always say that," Helen whined. "Why don't you ever tell me about the war?"

"Because you wouldn't like hearing about it," Thomas said curtly.

"Yes, I would," Helen argued. "I want to learn things."

"Not these kind of things."

"Yes, I do."

"No, you don't."

"Yes, I do."

"No, Helen," Thomas growled, "you don't."

"Please," Helen begged.

"No!" Thomas shouted. "I don't want to talk about it, understand? I just want to..."

Thomas lifted up his head and looked down the road. Noises were coming from the direction of the town.

"What's that?" Helen asked.

"Someone's coming," Thomas answered. He sat up and strained his eyes to see whether he could make out who was heading towards them. It looked as if 10 to 15 people were being led by a dog.

"Is that Joey's dog?" Helen questioned Thomas.

"I think so," Thomas answered. He could see the distinct orange color of Joey's dog, Taylor, even from far away. Thomas looked around nervously. The field was completely empty. Mary was still in the house and the rest of his family must have been off somewhere else. He was all alone.

Alfie sat upright. His ears perked up and he listened to the sound of people coming. Blue did the same only his left ear still remained bent down as always.

"Steady boys," Thomas urged his dogs. "We don't want any trouble."

Thomas looked around again at the empty field and back at the people. It was too late for him to run into the house. They had already seen him. Besides, he was tired of running and being called a coward.

"Look, there he is," someone called out from the group. Thomas could hear the commotion as the people became more excited. Some of them began to walk faster; a few of the boys even broke into a jog.

Thomas sat quietly and watched as the crowd headed towards him. From his distance he could see Joey, Peter, and Bobby, their fathers, as well as a few of their sisters, and about five or six other men from town.

"What do you think they want?" Helen asked softly.

"I don't know," Thomas answered, "but it can't be good."

Taylor began to bark and run towards Thomas. Alfie and Blue stood up and barked defensively.

"Easy, boys," Thomas commanded as he held both dogs gently by the scruff of the neck trying to calm them.

Taylor broke into a run and headed straight towards them. His fur flew back in the wind, his tail pointed straight back, and his teeth were shining. He barked several times as he ran. Thomas grabbed Helen's hand and took a step back while Alfie and Blue moved in front of Thomas and growled.

"Ruff, ruff, ruff," Taylor barked, running almost directly at Thomas. Suddenly, he turned and circled the group several times.

"Ruff!" Alfie responded in his high-pitched bark. Thomas was surprised that Alfie did not back away from Taylor, especially after the way Taylor had destroyed Alfie's leg.

"Ruff, Ruff!" Blue also barked in a much deeper tone.

At least Taylor's outnumbered, Thomas thought to himself.

"Calm down, boy, calm down!" Joey ordered Taylor as he approached. "There's no reason to get excited yet."

"See, there he is," Peter shouted and pointed. "I told you I saw him."

"I thought he never went outside," Peter's father said.

"He doesn't," Peter answered. "At least that is what his cousin Rachel said."

Rachel, Thomas growled to himself. *It figures that she would tell everyone. She hasn't spoken to me in over a week and she always has had a big mouth.*

"Well, he's here now," Joey announced.

The group approached Thomas and stood directly in front of him. Taylor continued to growl at Alfie and Blue while Joey lightly held him back.

"Hello, Thomas," Bobby's dad said in a friendly tone.

"Hi," Thomas replied quietly. His voice was shaky and his hands were sweating. He couldn't believe that all these people were here on a social call.

"How have you been?" Bobby's dad went on.

"Oh...okay," Thomas said.

"Been eating well?" a man in the back of the group said. It was Mr. Arnold from the grocery store.

"I suppose so," Thomas said.

"Much better than soldier food I bet," Mr. Arnold continued.

Thomas was starting to get an idea what this was all about.

"But that's not why you ran," Mr. Arnold went on. His eyes glowed fiercely and his jaw was firm and hard. "Is it, boy?"

Thomas took a step back. Helen squeezed his hand tighter.

"It would take more than that to turn him into a coward," Joey's father answered.

The group had completely encircled Thomas now. He looked left and right and noticed that the only thing between him and these people was the tree at his back.

"P-please," Thomas began. "Please, I don't want any trouble."

"No, city mouse," Joey snarled. "You just want to make fools of us."

"No!" Thomas shouted back.

Taylor jumped towards Thomas. Alfie and Blue barked fiercely.

"I never wanted to do that," Thomas said quickly as Joey grabbed Taylor to restrain him. He didn't want the dog to attack, at least not yet. "I never wanted to do anything like that. I only wanted to do the right thing."

"Running from your regiment and lying to your neighbors is right?" a woman scolded. It was Bobby's mother. "Who taught you your lessons, boy?"

Thomas didn't answer. His mind raced to think of a way out.

"Probably his older sister," Peter joked.

"Yeah," Bobby added with a laugh, "she may be stupid but she at least has some guts."

The boys laughed while the adults continued to stare.

"Don't call my sister stupid!" Helen suddenly shouted, running forward as she spoke and almost directly into Taylor.

"Ruff, ruff!" Taylor barked and snapped at Helen.

"Aaaahhh," Helen screamed, backing up behind Alfie and Blue.

"Even the little one's got some guts," Joey laughed as he pulled Taylor back again.

"Maybe Thomas is some weird kind of creature," Bobby suggested.

"That's it!" his father said laughing. "He's not really a boy. He's some kind of animal."

"An animal that runs real fast."

"Yeah, like a cheetah."

"That can change shape and look like a human."

"A pretty ugly one!"

"And smelly too."

Everyone began laughing. Thomas' face reddened as he became enraged. Tears started to swell up in his eyes.

"Oh look," Bobby teased, "I think we hurt the poor thing's feelings."

Thomas took a deep breath to control himself.

"Don't make it cry," Mr. Arnold jeered. "It might run away again."

"Stop it!" Helen yelled. She jumped forward in front of the dogs. "Stop making fun of my brother!"

Alfie and Blue got excited from Helen's yelling and began barking. Then Taylor began jumping and barking.

"Whoa, boy, whoa," Joey called to Taylor as he grabbed him harder to steady him. "Leave the girl alone."

Helen continued yelling. "He's not a coward! He's a good person and you can't make fun of him like this."

"Your brother is a chicken who runs from everything," Mr. Arnold shouted angrily as he stepped forward and accidently bumped into Joey. "He's a disgrace to everyone who ever put on a military uniform and until he is punished for his cowardice, the soul of my dear son will never rest!"

Taylor finally broke free of Joey's grip when Mr. Arnold bumped him. Helen jumped back in fright and Alfie and Blue who were already in a frenzy leaped forward.

"Ruff, ruff, ruff, ruff, ruff!" Alfie and Blue barked at Taylor to warn him.

Taylor did not cower. Instead, he stood his ground and growled at the dogs. Everyone started to back up as they realized that the dogs were about to fight. No one tried to calm the dogs.

Taylor jumped at Alfie who dodged out of the way and continued barking in his high-pitched bark. Again Taylor snapped and barked in anger trying to grab at Alfie, but this time the encounter was different. This time, Alfie had a friend: a big one.

Blue slammed into Taylor and sent him reeling. Taylor, surprised by Blue's strength, got up slowly and growled at Blue, trying to decide how to attack.

Blue barked his deep-threatening bark—a bark that Thomas had not heard since the battlefield. Taylor barked and then lunged at Blue.

Blue stood his ground, seemingly unafraid of Taylor who was the same size as Blue and certainly meaner. The two dogs snapped and bit at each other viciously, growling and panting. Taylor bit Blue on the ear and Blue snapped back on Taylor's neck. Taylor bit back again, catching Blue's nose, then Blue smashed Taylor in the head with his right forepaw.

A few of the boys started to cheer while most of the people were too stunned by the violence of the fight to speak. Thomas wanted the fight to stop, but the dogs were too ferocious for him to get close.

"Stop them! Stop them!" Helen screamed.

"C'mon, Taylor," Joey urged his dog. "Don't let that coward's dog get the best of you."

Taylor snapped at Blue again, this time his jaws grabbed only air. Blue swung backwards, turned, and leapt full force into Taylor's stomach. The blow sent both dogs down to the ground with Blue on top and Taylor scrambling underneath. Blue tightly clamped his jaw on Taylor's neck again. Taylor in a high-pitched yelp shook his head and his body trying to break free of Blue's grip, but Blue was too strong. Thomas remembered how Blue was able to hold a baseball in his teeth without breaking the skin and he realized Blue was just trying to pin Taylor. Taylor's rolling and smacking of his paws at Blue's snout only made Blue hold on that much harder. It looked as if Taylor would lose.

"Leave my dog alone!" Joey cried as he picked up a stone and hurtled it at Blue. The rock hit Blue in the face and knocked him senseless. Blood began to flow out of his eye as he slumped to the ground.

The crowd wasn't sure whether to cheer Joey for ending the fight or be disgusted with him for hurting the other dog. A brief moment of silence filled the air.

Alfie ran towards Taylor barking fiercely at him. The fight was not over.

Even though he was tired and weak from Blue's attack, Taylor barked back angrily at Alfie. Alfie stepped back.

Taylor lunged at Alfie's bad leg. Alfie was not fast enough to dodge the attack. He squealed as Taylor's teeth bit sharply.

"Alfie!" Thomas cried out.

Taylor, crazy with anger and pain from the last fight, was determined to take down Alfie. The little dog barked and cried trying to break free but it was useless.

"Stop it, stop!" Helen cried.

"Taylor," Joey commanded, trying to stop his dog.

The momentary distraction allowed Alfie to wiggle free as he limped back. Then Taylor turned and renewed his attack pouncing on Alfie's neck. He screamed as Taylor's jaws squeezed tightly on his neck.

"Stop it, stop it, stop it!" Helen screamed as she ran forward and began pounding her fists on Taylor's chest. "You're killing him!"

"Helen, no!" Thomas yelled. He recognized that Taylor was out of control and Helen was in real danger.

"Ruff, ruff," Taylor barked angrily at Helen. He turned towards her in anger. Alfie fell out of his jaws slumping to the ground. Helen screamed, turned, and ran.

"Ruff!" Taylor yelled as he ran after Helen.

"Taylor!" Joey cried in vain. "Stop!"

Helen saw that Taylor was about to reach for her. She screamed as Taylor leaped in the air to attack her.

"No!" Thomas screamed throwing his body in between Taylor and Helen. The dog, taken by surprise, landed on top of Thomas.

Thomas looked up. He was flat on his back with Taylor standing over him. The dog's eyes were glazed and his jaws were wide open with the saliva dripping down onto Thomas' chest. He could smell Taylor's rotten breath for the brief second before the dog bit.

"Taylor!" Joey cried futilely. Taylor opened his mouth wider and plunged his jaws towards Thomas' neck.

"No!" Thomas screamed as he extended his arm to block Taylor. The teeth clamped down on Thomas' arm.

"Aaaaahhh," Thomas screeched in pain as Taylor's teeth pierced his skin and his arm began to bleed.

Frustrated, Taylor opened his mouth to attack again. Reacting before Taylor could open his mouth completely, Thomas swung his other arm around Taylor's head forcing the jaws down again on Thomas' injured arm piercing his wound a second time. Thomas knew, however, that Taylor would not be able to do further damage to his arm if he could just keep the dog's jaws closed.

Taylor shrugged and squeezed in an attempt to free himself. Thomas pushed down on Taylor's head forcing the dog's jaws and teeth to close, knowing the dog would have difficultly putting forth more strength to open his mouth.

Running toward Taylor, Joey stopped and stared in disbelief at Thomas who, with his arm in Taylor's mouth, was wrestling with this out-of-control dog.

Thomas hugged Taylor's head even tighter, pulling it down towards his chest. Then, he lifted his leg and wrapped it over Taylor's body forming a complete body lock! Everyone then watched as Thomas simply held Taylor tightly while the dog vainly tried to wrestle itself free by moving its paws and wiggling its head. Thomas had all his weight on the dog as well as his strength to restrain him. Within a few moments, Taylor collapsed from exhaustion.

"Yaaay!" Helen cried as she ran to Thomas who was standing over Taylor with blood dripping from his arm. She hugged him as hard as she could. "You did it, Thomas, you did it," she cried. "You saved me."

Helen continued to hug and kiss Thomas while he turned and looked at his dogs.

"Alfie!" Thomas cried, running over to his fallen pet. "What has he done to you?"

Alfie lifted up his head and stared at Thomas. His eyes were sad and his tail wagged slowly back and forth. A pool of blood was at his neck and his feet. It didn't look good.

"Alfie!" Thomas cried again. He pulled the dog's head up gently onto his lap and began to stroke him gently. "Take it easy, boy, take it easy. It'll be alright."

"Is he going to be O.K.?" Helen said softly.

"I don't know," Thomas answered. "I don't know."

"Let me look at him," Bobby's mother suddenly said. "Maybe I can help."

Thomas looked back at the woman whose eyes were soft with a tear slowly running down her cheek. She bent down and inspected Alfie's wounds.

"What you did back there was a brave thing," the woman said softly to Thomas. "I don't think anyone will be calling you a coward after today."

Thomas tried to respond but he didn't know what to say. He didn't even care right now. Alfie's eyes were drifting deeper and deeper into his forehead, and his tail was slowly losing its wag. Helen began to cry.

CHAPTER TWELVE

THE INVASION

Thomas stood over Alfie's grave. He didn't know what to say. He had loved Alfie so much. He was the only one who accepted Thomas for what he was and had loved Thomas no matter what he did. And now he was gone.

Blue wagged his tail slowly and looked at Thomas. It was clear that Blue knew what had happened to Alfie but even so he seemed more concerned with the pain Thomas felt than his own. He rubbed his head against Thomas' leg, whimpered a little and continued to stare into Thomas' eyes. The bruise from the rock that Joey threw was still puffy. Mary had told Thomas that it would heal fine.

Mary had run outside after the fight was already over and the neighbors had gone their own way. They had left without a word, with their heads hung down. Strangely enough, Alfie's death and Thomas' rescue of Helen from the crazed dog had seemed to quiet everyone's criticism of him. No one called him a coward anymore. Now, if only he could do what he had to do.

"I'm sorry, Thomas," Mary said to him as she approached the grave. "I know how much you loved him."

"Thanks," Thomas replied softly. He didn't feel much like talking.

"I noticed you packed up your haversack," Mary added after an awkward silence. She could tell that Thomas did not want to talk about Alfie.

"Yeah," Thomas replied slowly. "I'm going back."

"To the regiment?" Mary wondered.

"Yeah," Thomas said simply. "I got nothing left to stay for here. I might as well go."

"You're not going just because of this, are you?" Mary asked. She was pleased that Thomas had finally made a decision, yet she still was afraid of what might happen to him. If he went off to war, she wanted it to be for the right reasons.

"No," Thomas explained. "Not really. I been thinking about what David said. I been thinking about what you said. I even been thinking about what the neighbors have said."

Mary looked at him in surprise.

"I have been running," Thomas admitted. "I've been running from being picked on, running from family, running from the farm, and running from the war. But I'm tired of running. I'm tired of feeling like a coward."

"You're not a coward," Mary said firmly.

"I know," Thomas agreed. His certainty surprised Mary. "I proved that to myself during the fight with Taylor. When something is really important to me, I don't run. I am as brave as anyone."

"I know," Mary said smiling. "I've always known that. And I'm glad you know that too."

"I just wish Alfie didn't have to die for me to learn this," Thomas said sadly, staring down at the grave again.

"Me too," Mary said.

Thomas turned away from the grave and looked at Mary.

"Well, I guess this is good-bye," he said sadly.

"No, it's not," Mary argued. Thomas looked at her in confusion. There was a strange silence as Mary's mouth began to show a smirk.

"I'm going with you!" she explained.

"What?" Thomas exclaimed. "You can't go with me, I'm going off to fight!"

"I know that," Mary cried impatiently. "I'm not going to be a soldier. What did you think, that I would be some woman who disguises herself as a man just to fight?"

"Well, I...uh," Thomas mumbled.

"Women don't have to dress as men to help out in this war, you know," Mary began. This was obviously a sore subject for her, speaking in a tone of voice as if she had said this many times in the past. The anger and bitterness in her voice weren't so much directed at Thomas as it was directed at the war in general. "Everyone seems to think that if you are not a soldier then you are not doing anything. They think only the fighting is what matters."

Thomas stood and listened. He knew better than to interrupt Mary when she was giving one of her speeches. He reached down and patted Blue while he waited for her to continue.

"Well, you boys couldn't fight without us," Mary continued after a short pause. "We have made your clothes, organized your recruitment, cleaned up your camps, and tended to the wounded."

"I know that, Mary," Thomas finally said. "Why are you telling me this now?"

"Because I'm tired of being here," Mary whined. "We may be getting some things done but I want to do more."

"Like what?"

"I don't know," Mary responded. "Work for the sanitary commission and inspect the camps, help with the wounded. I don't know, just something more."

"You're not old enough to be a nurse."

"I know that," Mary replied. "But I'm old enough to help out. After all, if you can do it, why can't I?"

Thomas looked at Mary. He didn't really have any argument there. If he was in the army, why couldn't she help too? She was older than he was, and even if she was a girl, he had already seen and heard about women in the camps taking care of the wounded and making sure that the camp was healthy. The way Mary always took care of his cuts and bruises, she'd be a natural.

"But what about Aunt Patricia?" Thomas suddenly realized. "What will she say?"

"What can she say?" Mary said smartly. "I'm not her daughter and she certainly doesn't treat me like she wants me around. She'll be glad to see me go."

She was probably right about that too, Thomas thought to himself. Aunt Patricia never hid her dislike for Mary and always played favorites with her actual daughters, Rachel and Jamie.

"Well, O.K.," Thomas said after a few more seconds of thinking. "I don't see any reason why you can't go. I probably couldn't stop you anyway and I could use some company."

"Hooray," Mary cheered as she jumped into Thomas' arms and hugged him around the neck. "Thank you, Thomas, thank you."

"You just gotta get lost when we get near my regiment," Thomas warned. He pushed Mary back and stared at her to show how serious he was.

"Don't worry," Mary said quickly. "As soon as we get near the troops, I'll go find the sanitary commission or hospital tent. No one will know your sister came with you."

The next day, Mary and Thomas set out to find Thomas' regiment. He was a little worried that they would punish him for being a deserter but he had already decided that he would accept whatever punishment the army gave to him. It would help him deal with the guilt of running in the first place and it probably wouldn't be half as bad as the prison where Mark was. Besides, with the way the war was going, they needed every man they could get. Maybe they'd just let him off the hook since he was so young.

Helen was upset to see her brother and sister go. She cried the entire time they said good-bye. Mary almost decided to put off leaving and stay with her until Aunt Patricia nudged her out the door. She promised she would take care of Helen. With Mary out of the house, she claimed, it would be that much easier.

The trip to Washington, D.C., was uneventful except for the argument Thomas had with the train conductor. He was not about to let a dog on the train and he stubbornly blocked the entrance until Thomas explained that

Blue was the regiment's mascot and he needed to get back as quickly as possible.

They had chosen to go to Washington because Thomas' regiment was now stationed somewhere in the area. As part of the Army of the Potomac, the regiment was in the midst of regrouping after the terrible disaster at Second Bull Run. With all of the chaos of wartime, Thomas thought the best place to find his unit was to start at the capital. He did not want to wait for a letter from his uncle telling him where the army was. By the time they arrived there the army would be somewhere else.

They arrived in Washington by the second week in September. The moment they stepped off the train, they sensed something was wrong. The town was chaotic with people hurrying everywhere and talking quickly and anxiously. Carriages sped down the dirt streets and horses raced by so fast that it became dangerous to even cross the street.

"What's going on?" Thomas said to a stranger who was hurrying past him in the opposite direction. The man completely ignored Thomas and continued on his way.

"What's going on?" Thomas repeated to two or three more passersby, but they too hurried past. Finally, Thomas grabbed an older looking man by the sleeve and held onto him as tight as he could.

"Excuse me, sir," Thomas said politely. "What is going on? Why is the city so crazy?"

The man looked down at Thomas' hand still holding his sleeve. He glared at Thomas.

"I would think a soldier would know the answer to that," he said angrily.

"I...uh...I," Thomas stuttered. "I've been on leave. I just got back."

"Well, you better get to your regiment quickly," the man snapped as he pulled his sleeve from Thomas' grasp. "General Lee's taken his army north into Maryland. It's an invasion."

Thomas' arm fell to his side and he took a step backwards.

"An invasion?" he repeated under his breath. "An invasion?"

Mary stopped another passerby.

"Excuse me, sir," she said politely. "Is it true that General Lee has invaded the North?"

"It sure is, young lady," the man replied a little more friendly and a little less in a hurry. "People are saying that he wants to show the North that they don't have a chance. He may even get England and France to join in."

"England and France?" Mary repeated.

"Yup," he said simply. "They have stayed out of it so far either because of our blockade or because of the South's slavery system. But lots of people think that if Lee has a good victory, then they will join the war on the South's side."

"My Lord," Thomas gasped. "That would be a disaster."

"Sure would," the man agreed. "We wouldn't stand a chance then."

"W-where is he now?" Thomas managed to ask.

"Don't really know," he replied. "Some say that he's in the northwestern part of the state and headed to Pennsylvania."

"Pennsylvania?" Mary gasped. "That's my home!"

"Well, maybe you should get back there, little lady," the man said finally as he began to walk away. "And you should get to your regiment, soldier."

Chapter Thirteen

Three Cigars

Thomas and Mary stood staring at each other in shock. What would they do now?

"I've got to find my unit," Thomas finally spoke. "I've got to help."

"I'll go with you," Mary added.

"O.K.," Thomas answered. His mind was already racing to figure out what to do next. Mary would be a help certainly in locating his unit. He'd leave her as soon as they got close to it.

"Let's try the war department," Thomas suggested.

Thomas and Mary made their way to the war department as quickly as possible. They were shocked at what they had heard and both of them mumbled back and forth to each other.

"What if Lee makes it to Pennsylvania?" Mary wondered aloud.

"He won't," Thomas said firmly.

"How do you know?"

"I...I don't," Thomas replied.

"He hasn't lost a battle yet," Mary said after another second or two.

"I know," Thomas replied.

The war department was in absolute chaos with soldiers and civilians running everywhere and yelling. It seemed that no one knew exactly what to do or where to go. Thomas and Mary were barely able to get inside. All they could find out was that the army was somewhere near the town of Frederick, Maryland.

They were able to get out of the city fairly quickly and make their way towards the Potomac. Frederick was not that far from the river, and they felt that if they could get a ride upstream for a while, then they would be that much closer to the army. Thomas hoped that they found the right army. It would not be any fun to make his return to a Confederate prison.

"This is as far as I can take you," the owner of the boat said after several hours. The man had been willing to take them in his small boat up the Potomac as far as the Monocacy River but he was afraid to go any further. "You'll have to head the rest of the way on foot."

Thomas and Mary got off the boat slowly. Blue simply leapt right onto shore.

"Sure is a fine dog you have there," the man said as he pushed his boat away from the shore.

"Thanks," Thomas said simply. "And thanks for the ride."

"No problem," the man said waving. "Maryland may be a border state, but that doesn't mean that I'm no less loyal than the rest of you. Besides," he went on as he began to row away, "if those rebels keep going, they're libel to destroy everything in the area, including my farm."

"Well, Mary," Thomas said, turning away from the river and towards his sister, "I think this is where we should say good-bye."

"So soon?" Mary complained.

"You heard the man," Thomas said. "The Confederates are all over the place. A group of 'em were in this area not more than a day or two ago."

"I know," she replied. "I just wanted to make sure that you found your unit."

"Don't worry about me," Thomas replied. "There are Federal units swarming in the area. I heard something about the XII Corps and the II Corps."

"You're II Corps, right?" Mary asked.

"Yeah," Thomas answered simply. "So I really should get going. Why don't you head into Keedysville and talk to the local people there. They probably know where you can find a hospital or sanitation unit."

"O.K.," Mary said slowly. She knew Thomas was right but she didn't want to leave him. This could be the last time she ever saw him. "Take care of yourself, Thomas," she said finally. "You may not be a coward but you're not invulnerable either."

"Don't worry," Thomas laughed. "I'll keep my head down."

The two of them hugged. It was a long, strong hug and Thomas did not want it to end. He loved Mary, more than he ever realized. She had been his friend, his protector, his sister, and even his mother when there was no one else to be there for him. Now that she was here in Maryland, he not only had to worry about himself, he also had to worry about her.

"You be careful too," Thomas said at last. He gave her one last squeeze and pushed her out to arm's length. "Just because you don't wear a uniform doesn't mean they won't shoot you."

"I will," Mary promised. "Good-bye."

"Goodbye," Thomas replied.

He stood and watched Mary walk away.[1]

"C'mon, Blue," he said finally. "Let's go."

They walked for several hours. Frederick was at least a half-day's walk and it was already late in the afternoon. As dusk began to approach, Thomas looked for a place to stay for the night.

There were many signs of soldiers in the area, so he wanted to be careful about what he said or did. He certainly didn't want to sleep in the open and he didn't have that much money to pay for a room. Fortunately, as he neared town he noticed a deserted camp ahead that must have been used by soldiers at some point during the war.

Thomas walked slowly to the cabins. They seemed to have been made from the local trees and pieced together quickly. The cabins were long and rectangular, the type used for many soldiers at a time. Clearly this had been a camp for a regiment or even larger. Thomas looked around in each cabin and in the trees around the area to make sure no one was there, friend or foe. Finally, after checking the camp for almost an hour, he realized that it was deserted and he settled down for the night.

The next day Thomas awoke early and ate his last bit of bread. *Better find something else soon,* he said to himself. "C'mon, Blue."

The two of them rose quickly and headed away from the camp. It was a pleasant, warm day and Thomas couldn't help but watch the trees swaying in the breeze

---

1. To find out what happens to Mary be sure to read book 5 of the Young Heroes of History series entitled *No Girls Allowed.*

and listen to the birds singing in the air. September was one of the most beautiful months of the year he noticed. The trees had not yet lost their leaves, and the summer heat and humidity had pretty much disappeared. All that remained was the warm air and the blue sky.

After several hours of walking, Thomas was beginning to get tired. "Let's look for a place to rest, Blue," he said.

Thomas saw a field of clover up ahead that looked like a perfect place to lie down. There were visible traces that soldiers had camped there recently but it was currently unoccupied. Thomas found a place in the shade on a grassy slope near a rail fence to lay down and rest. As he lay on his back, Thomas looked up at the slowly moving clouds.

"I see a cat," Thomas said to Blue. The dog raised his head in interest then lay back down. Thomas smiled. *I think I'll try to find a dragon for Helen,* he said to himself. *Who knows, maybe she's looking at the same clouds I am.*

Thomas lay in the grass for a while resting while Blue began to get antsy and began sniffing around the grass.

"Cut that out, Blue," Thomas scolded. "There's nothing here."

Blue continued to sniff instinctively as if he smelled something.

"Whatcha smell, Blue?" Thomas wondered as he sat up and looked around.

Blue stopped, put his nose to the grass, opened his mouth, and picked up something.

"Hey, boy," Thomas called. "Bring it over."

Blue turned and ran over to Thomas placing the item in Thomas' outstretched hand.

"What's this?" Thomas wondered aloud.

In his hand was a yellowish paper package. Thomas opened it up and found three small cigars.

"Well, what do you know?" Thomas said happily. "I guess you did find something, Blue."

Thomas carefully sniffed and examined the cigars. They didn't seem to be special in anyway, but he could always use them.

"Hey, what's this?" Thomas said out loud as he opened a piece of paper wrapped around the cigars. "It looks like a letter."

Thomas read it:

Headquarters, Army of Northern Virginia
Sept. 9th 1862

"Holy!" Thomas whistled. "It's a letter from Lee's army!"

Thomas couldn't believe what he was holding. Were these actually orders from General Lee? He read on.

Special Orders No. 191
III. The army will resume its march to-morrow...

"Oh my God!" Thomas shouted as his eyes scanned the paper. "It is...it is a letter from General Lee!" He scanned it some more. "It gives the whole details of his invasion plan! This could save the whole country and end the war! I've got to..."

Noises came from the woods. It sounded like troops were approaching.

Oh no! Thomas thought to himself in a panic. *Maybe the Confederates who dropped this were heading back!*

Thomas looked around and saw some bushes near the fence. He stuffed the cigars and the letter back in the envelope.

"C'mon, Blue," he said as he rushed towards the bushes to hide. "Let's see who they are first."

As Thomas watched, soldiers dressed in blue began to walk out into the field. At first there were just a few, but soon over a hundred of them had begun to spread out into the field and lay down to rest.

"At least they're Union soldiers," Thomas said to Blue, breathing a sigh of relief. "Looks like a whole regiment. I was afraid that...oh no!" Thomas shouted, reaching into his pockets and looking around on the grass. "The letter, I dropped it!"

Thomas peered out on the field to the spot where the letter lay. Next to it, four soldiers sat down to relax.

Now what do I do? Thomas wondered as he carefully watched the soldiers, never once taking his eyes off the envelope.

One of the men lay on the ground right next to the envelope. He stretched his arms and glanced in its direction. He rolled over and picked it up.

"What is it?" another soldier asked, who saw him pick up the package. He looked like he might be a sergeant, Thomas noticed.

"An envelope."

"Hand it to me."

The soldier handed it to the sergeant and as he did so, the cigars fell onto the grass. There was some commotion as the soldiers smiled at the sight of the cigars and began looking for a match. Thomas never moved. He kept his eyes on the sergeant who still held the letter in his hand.

"Oh no!" Thomas cried as he realized the man was about to crumple the paper. "He must think it's just wrapping. "Wait! Wait!" Thomas cried as he ran out of the bushes with his arms flailing in the air. "Don't drop that, don't drop that!"

All of the men turned in surprise and grabbed their guns.

"Don't shoot!" Thomas cried. "I'm one of you."

The men slowly lowered their weapons as Thomas approached.

"What are you doing here, soldier?" the sergeant asked angrily.

"I'm looking for my regiment," Thomas said quickly, "but that's not important now. Look at that paper," Thomas urged. "It's a letter from General Lee himself."

"Huh?" the sergeant said as he looked down at the paper and began to read it. The other soldiers stood up and peered over his shoulder. "You're right," he said after a few minutes. "This looks like his whole battle plan."

"I better take this to Captain Kop," the sergeant said as he turned and walked away. "You better come with me, boy."

Thomas followed the sergeant as he took it to his captain and then on to Colonel Colgrove, the regimental commander. Thomas' legs bounded up and down with each step, and he couldn't stop himself from smiling. The excitement almost made him burst. He had actually found the papers describing Lee's whole battle plan! Not just a piece, but the whole darn plan! Now General McClellan could form a new plan and catch Lee completely by surprise.

"My God," Colonel Colgrove whistled after he too finished reading the letter. "This really is from Lee. And you say this boy here found it?" he asked the captain.

"Yes, he did, sir," the captain began to explain. Unfortunately, he was interrupted by the sound of a horse fast approaching. It raced toward them and stopped suddenly in front of them.

"General Kimball, sir," the colonel said to the man riding the horse as he and the captain saluted. Thomas followed their lead and saluted as well. "You have to see this. This boy found a letter from General Lee himself, sir," the colonel explained as he handed the letter to the general.

General Kimball dismounted from his horse and read the letter. Then he turned to Thomas.

"You found this, boy?" the general asked in a suspicious tone. It would not be the first time that false information had been passed on within the army.

"Y-yes, sir," Thomas said nervously. "Actually my dog found it, sir, he..."

"Your dog?" General Kimball repeated in surprise. He looked at Blue standing silently at Thomas' side, wagging his tail and sticking out his tongue. Blue had no idea of the importance of what he had just done. "What unit are you in?" the general asked Thomas abruptly.

"Uh-uh," Thomas stuttered. Even though he had found this letter the general would not want to hear that he was a deserter. "The California Regiment," Thomas finally answered.

"California?" General Kimball repeated. "What are you doing here? No, never mind. I don't have time for that. I have to get this to General Williams."

"General Williams?" Thomas repeated.

"Twelfth Corps commander," General Kimball explained. "You may have just saved the army and the country, private?" he looked quizzically at Thomas. After a slight pause Thomas realized that the general was asking him for his name.

"Thomas Adams," he answered.

"Well, Private Adams," the general continued, "I suppose you're kind of a hero."

A hero? Thomas thought to himself. *A hero. Wow! I'll be famous, I'll be...oh no! oh no! if that happens everyone will want to know what I was doing here. They'll know I ran away and the whole country will find out I was a coward!*

"Wait, wait!" Thomas called to the general who was turning his horse. The general stopped and turned around to face Thomas.

"Please, sir," Thomas began, "I don't want to be a hero. I just want to be a soldier."

"Hmmmm," the general responded. "That's very noble of you, son." He put his hand to his chin and stroked his black beard. "I suppose we could give the credit to those men who found you," he thought out loud. "Doesn't really matter to me. But at least let me put a good word in for you with your superior, General Howard."[2]

"O.K.," Thomas smiled. He realized that a good word could help him get back in with the regiment.

"Well then," General Kimball said with a wave, "I'm off to give old General Lee a real surprise. Thanks again, son."

---

2. A copy of Special Orders No. 191, which described Lee's invasion plan, was, indeed, found in the grass south of Frederick, Maryland, on the morning of September 13, 1862. It was discovered by Sergeant Bloss, and Privates Mitchell, Bur, and Vance of the 27th Indiana Infantry Regiment.

**CONFEDERATE GENERAL
ROBERT E. LEE,
COMMANDER OF THE ARMY OF
NORTHERN VIRGINIA**
National Archives

**UNION GENERAL
GEORGE B. MCCLELLAN,
COMMANDER OF THE
ARMY OF THE POTOMAC**
National Archives

Chapter Fourteen

The Return

Thomas stood at the edge of the trees and watched the men in his unit. He still couldn't believe how friendly the commander of his regiment had been once Thomas finally found them. The desertion had been forgotten and Thomas had been welcomed back with open arms.

"We'll need every man we can get for this fight," Colonel Wistar had said to Thomas with a pat on the back. *It was amazing what a good word from the right person could do,* Thomas thought. Maybe it was because Thomas was still a kid or that Colonel Wistar was just a kind man. It didn't really matter. As long as he had been allowed to return to his original company, Thomas didn't care why he had been let off the hook.

Watching his old friends playing cards, cleaning their rifles, or just joking around, he wondered if this had all been a big mistake. Colonel Wistar had forgiven him, but his friends still might resent his leaving, might call him a coward, or might not even talk to him. Thomas shuddered as he realized how uncomfortable the next scene would be. He took a deep breath and walked into the camp.

"Hi, guys," he said casually with a wave of his hand.

Some of the men turned and looked at him while others continued what they were doing.

"Thomas!" Chris shouted in excitement. His blond hair was all over his head as usual and the baseball that he always held was firmly in his hand. He was still finding time to practice his pitching, throwing the ball to anyone who would catch it. "I thought we'd never see you again," Chris said as he threw one more pitch. "Hey, guys, look who's back, it's Thomas!"

More of the men stopped what they were doing and began to stand up. Thomas looked intently at their faces, wondering what their reactions might be. Some of them looked curious, others looked genuinely glad to see him, and a few looked angry.

"What are you doing back here?" one of the soldiers from Chester's old baseball team said gruffly. He spit a piece of tobacco on the ground and scowled directly at Thomas.

"Yeah," the soldier playing cards with him added, "the last time we saw you was at the bluff."

Everyone stood quiet for a moment as the terrible memories of Ball's Bluff returned.

"I...I came back to help," Thomas replied after the awkward silence. He had rehearsed what he would say over and over again but even so the words still had trouble coming out.

"Hmmph," the first soldier said. "I heard you ran away."

"I, uh, I," Thomas stuttered.

"Hey!" a loud voice suddenly called. All eyes turned to see another soldier walking into the camp. It was Chester, loudmouthed, obnoxious Chester. "What are you doing back here?" Chester shouted. "And why'd you bring the dog with you?"

"Dog?" a few of the men mumbled.

"Blue!" Chris and several of Thomas' old baseball teammates shouted as they realized that the dog was sitting calmly by Thomas' side. "How you doing, boy?" they called as they ran to the dog and began petting him. Blue sat up happily, stuck out his tongue, wagged his tail, and let the soldiers pat him.

"Hey, guys, take it easy," Thomas said laughing. "You'll rub off all his fur."

"I thought we lost him back at the bluff," Chris said as he scratched Blue behind the ears. "No one had seen him or said a word about him."

"Would have been better if we had lost him," Chester interrupted. He still hadn't forgiven the dog for embarrassing him and making him lose the baseball game. "The dog's just a nuisance."

"Ignore him, guys," Chris said before anyone could start a fight. "He's just a mean old cuss. Isn't he, Blue?" Chris said affectionately to the dog as he scratched him even harder.

"Rrrrrr," Chester grumbled as he walked away. "Stupid dog."

Thomas smiled as he watched Chester sit down with his buddies. Everyone was too busy playing with Blue to even realize that Thomas was standing there.

"Here, Blue," Larry called. He had been one of the outfielders on the team. He picked up a stick on the ground and threw it. "Go get it, boy, go get it."

Thomas sat down on a rock in disbelief. It was just like old times all over again. Chester and his group assembled on their own, and the other guys playing and running with Blue. It was as if he had never left.

At the same time, Thomas realized that things had changed: people were missing. Thomas thought about Mark in the Richmond prison and lowered his head. He'd missed a lot while he was gone.

The regiment had experienced many battles since he had run away. They had been involved in the invasion of Virginia and McClellan's attempt to take Richmond, the Confederacy's capital. They had marched all over the area, trying to find Lee's army or to guard Washington. During this time, many men had been lost or wounded. Thomas hung his head in sadness, thinking of the people that he would never see again.

The playing continued for almost another hour. Some of the men lost interest and continued with what they had been doing before Thomas had arrived. A few soldiers who had been close to Thomas talked with him for a while but no one really seemed to care about that day on the bluff. It was as if they all understood what had happened and were content to simply forget about it.

Everyone, that is, except for Chester and his friends who never moved from their spot the entire time. They continued playing cards, chewing tobacco, and staring at Thomas with a look of disgust.

The next several days, everyone was anxious, knowing that the next battle could possibly decide the outcome of the war. With the secret plans in his hands, McClellan realized that if he struck quickly, he could surprise Lee while his army was still separated.[1]

Tensions ran high and more than once there was a fight among the men. Generally, everyone worked

---

1. Lee had divided his forces and sent some troops under General Thomas "Stonewall" Jackson to attack Harpers Ferry, Virginia. He also sent some troops under General Ambrose P. Hill to guard South Mountain in Maryland.

together to prepare the regiment for battle. Then, four days after Thomas had found the secret plans, the soldiers were awakened at two in the morning for an inspection of their cartridge boxes. It was still dark and the air was still. The animals of the woods were silent and only some fireflies could be seen near the tents. A few soldiers wandered around the camp but most of the men were just waking up. Like Thomas, they sat and waited nervously for instructions.

"What's going on?" Thomas asked Chris who had just finished counting his cartridges.

"Don't know, but it's got to be something big. Here," Chris said as he gave Thomas some more ammunition. "They're stuffing us with ammo. Put some of it in your pockets."

"Whew," Thomas whistled as he looked at the pile of bullets in his hands. He had to stuff the bullets in his pockets with one hand while using the other hand to pick up those that had fallen to the ground. "They must be expecting a big battle."

"Yeah," Chris agreed. He made no attempt to discuss the upcoming fight because it was too uncomfortable to talk about before a battle.

Thomas stretched his arms and yawned. Chris did the same. "I'm going to try to get more sleep," Chris said in between another yawn.

Thomas watched Chris return to his tent. A few soldiers had followed Chris' lead to try to fall asleep again. Others grumbled about waking up so early with nothing to do but wait for the next order. Thomas looked at the thousands of stars shining in the sky. Crickets and frogs chirped and croaked in the distance. Thomas looked at Blue sleeping comfortably in the grass. Sitting down next to him and gently rubbing the dog's fur, Thomas talked out loud: "Well, Blue, I guess this is it. I guess this is where I find out just what I am made of. I wonder if I'll get shot? I wonder if I'll die? I wonder if I'll even have the guts to stay and fight?

Thomas took a stick and drew absent-mindedly in the dirt with it while lost in his thoughts.

I can't run this time. This war means everything: the life of the country, the freedom of the slaves, everything. I can't run. I won't run. I won't. I don't care how bad it gets, I have got to stay and be brave. I've got to show everyone that I am not a coward and that I'm grown up now, that I can do whatever they do.

Thomas sighed. He looked around at the soldiers sitting quietly.

I wish Mary were here, or David, or even Mom and Dad. Gosh, I could use a friendly face right about now.

"Hey, kid," a voice suddenly interrupted.

Thomas looked up to see loudmouthed, obnoxious Chester standing over him. His heart sank and he looked back down at the ground. *This must be the least friendly face in the regiment,* Thomas thought.

"Whatcha doing?" Chester asked as he sat on the ground next to Thomas.

"Just sitting here," Thomas admitted.

"Thinking about the fight?" Chester wondered.

"Sort of," Thomas admitted. He hoped that if he showed no interest in talking, Chester would leave him alone.

"Me too," Chester admitted.

Thomas was surprised at the seriousness in Chester's voice. For once, he didn't sound mean or obnoxious. His voice seemed to be filled with worry and concern.

"This is going to be a big one," Chester continued, pushing some leaves to the side. "I can feel it. Probably bigger than any we've ever been in."

"Probably," Thomas agreed.

"A lot of us ain't going to make it," Chester admitted. "You, me, who knows what will happen!"

Thomas stopped playing with the stick and looked into Chester's eyes. Thomas had never seen him so serious.

"I, um, I," Chester mumbled and stuttered. "I've been talking with the guys, you know, the ones from my team. At first we were angry at you for doing what you did. Then we started thinking about how you came back and all." He paused.

Thomas stared anxiously at Chester, waiting for him to continue.

"Well, I, uh," he stuttered again. "I just want you to know that I think you did a brave thing coming back here after what happened."

Thomas' eyes lit up and his ears stood at attention. He couldn't believe what he was hearing.

"A lot of guys would have never had the guts to face us again," Chester explained. "But you came back to help out, not knowing what we would do or how we would even treat you."

"You're not angry at me for running from the bluff?" Thomas dared to ask.

"Nahhh, not really," Chester admitted. "We all ran. We all acted crazy, stumbling over each other while trying to get away. You just ran a little farther, that's all."

"But what if I run again?" Thomas said frankly. For some reason he felt as if he could say anything to Chester. Maybe it was because Chester had been candid with him.

"You won't," Chester said firmly. "Guys like you who face their fears don't panic a second time. You know what to expect. You know what it's going to be like, and you came back. Heck, it can't be any worse than the bluff."

"I guess not," Thomas agreed.

"Besides," Chester said with a grin, "I got a feeling that Blue wouldn't let you run even if you wanted to."

Chapter Fifteen

The West Woods

After several hours of waiting in the dark, Thomas' regiment had been ordered to move towards the town of Sharpsburg. All morning they had listened to the exchange of small weapons fire and artillery shells. After crossing Antietam Creek, the regiment lined up and awaited their orders to advance. As he listened to the sounds of the battle not far away, Thomas knew that he would be involved in some heavy fighting, but nothing could have prepared him for the sight that lay before him.

Rebel and Union soldiers lay everywhere in the huge cornfield. Whole rows of dead men lay behind demolished rail fences, stumps, clumps of bushes, or any object which offered some protection from the rain of bullets and cannon shells. Their bodies were stuck in all kinds of positions, as if they were frozen. Thomas could tell by the looks on their faces that they had made a most desperate and determined fight but were shot down in their tracks.[1] Without any time to dwell

---

1. This is how 2nd Lieutenant John Rogers, Company G, 71st Pennsylvania, described the battle.

on this gruesome scene, however, Thomas was ordered to cross the field as quickly as possible. He had trouble stepping around the scores of mangled bodies. Many of the rebel soldiers in their last agony asked Thomas and his comrades not to tread on them. Although some of the wounded and dying asked for water, the regiment had no time to stop and help the dying soldiers.[2]

The Confederates continued to fire upon the regiment as they crossed the cornfield and climbed over a fence. Thomas kept his head down and noticed a few men fall but the attack appeared to do little damage.

As they crossed the field and headed into the woods, Thomas began to get more nervous. The shocking scenes of death hadn't bothered him as much as the eeriness of the woods. In the open field it was much easier to see what was going on. Even though it was easier to get hit, Thomas preferred that to the confusion he was now feeling. With the many rocks, trees, and leaves, the enemy could not be seen until they were upon you. Worse still was the fact that some of the regiment and most of the Federal forces were on the other side of a rock outcropping, separating Thomas' company along with many others.

Gunshots were heard from ahead. The men looked around to try to understand what was going on but the only thing they could see were rocks, trees, and the backs of the soldiers in front of them. Because it didn't seem to be too serious of a threat, Colonel Wistar ordered the men to lie down and rest so that they didn't get hit by a stray bullet or accidently fire into the backs of their comrades.

---

2. This is a description of the battle scene by Lieutenant Benjamin Hibbs, Company D, 71st Pennsylvania.

"What's going on?" Chris asked Thomas as he covered his blond head. A cannon shell had just landed a few feet away from him and had showered the men with dirt.

"I don't know," Thomas shouted over the noise. "I can't see a thing."

"At least most of the shells seem to be aimed over our heads," Chris cried, covering his ears. "I just hope it stays that way."

"Yeah," Thomas agreed as he reached over to pet Blue. The dog seemed undisturbed by the chaos around him and was sitting calmly next to Thomas.

"That dog is amazing," Larry added as he looked up from the dirt. "Doesn't anything ever faze him."

"Not that I've seen," shouted Thomas. "In fact, you should have seen him one time when he got in this fight with another dog named Taylor. He was so confident that..."

A whistle scream from a cannon shell pierced the air. Then an explosion ripped through Thomas' body. He covered his ears.

"Aaaahhhh!" Larry screamed.

"He's hit, he's hit," Chris yelled.

More screams as gunshots and artillery filled the air.

"On your feet!" Thomas heard someone shout. "On your feet!"

Thomas jumped to his feet and looked around. He saw Colonel Wistar shouting and waving his arms. He looked towards where he was pointing and saw a mass of men running towards them in terror.

"Hold fast, men," the order came down the line. "They're our own troops!"

Thomas gripped his rifle hard and flashed his bayonet forward. If these men ran through Thomas' regiment, everything would collapse and no one would know what to do or where to go.

"What could be making them run like that?" Chris wondered aloud.

The soldiers in front kept running right at them. Their faces were portraits of horror as they ran blindly from whatever was attacking them. Thomas began to sweat as he realized that they might run right into his bayonet! Blue barked loudly and fiercely at them, trying to warn them. It amazed Thomas that the dog was able to tell the difference between friend and foe in this chaotic mess.

"Aaaahhh!" many of them were screaming as they ran.

Thomas almost got run over. Fortunately, enough of the panic-stricken soldiers saw the bayonets in time and ran around the regiment. Only a few men bowled into the line of soldiers still holding firm. Thomas strained his eyes forward, trying to see what they were running from.

Cannon shells exploded from all around.

"They're behind us!" someone shouted.

Thomas looked back. Smoke was everywhere. He could see almost nothing. Bullets and cannon shells landed in every direction. Men were screaming. Blue was barking. Explosions hit everywhere.

"We have to get out of here!" Chris shouted.

"Hold on, hold on!" Thomas shouted.

"But we're surrounded!" Chris argued back.

"We've go to hold on!" Thomas yelled angrily. "If we run now it will be Ball's Bluff all over again! We can't panic, not now."

Chris looked back nervously. Men were dying around him and he had no idea which way to shoot. "Alright, alright," he agreed quickly. "But we have to do something."

"I know," Thomas agreed, "but what?"

"Wheel left, wheel left!" Colonel Wistar's voice suddenly rang out over the explosions. "The enemy is flanking us!"

Thomas and Chris looked to their left and began to move. Shots overwhelmed the men. Three men to Thomas' right fell. Two soldiers behind him screamed out in pain. But the men continued to listen to orders.

"The colonel's been hit!" someone shouted.

The line stopped wheeling left as Lieutenant Rogers ran to the colonel's side.

"Keep moving, keep moving!" someone shouted amid the noise.

The sounds of the gunshots, the cannon explosions, men shouting orders and screaming were so loud that no one could hear the orders being given. Thomas looked down at Blue and saw him barking but he could barely hear him.

"Stay down, boy!" Thomas tried to command him.

A bullet knocked off Thomas' hat and another glanced off his bayonet. The vibration caused his hands to shake and he dropped his rifle.

"Blue!" Thomas heard someone yell as he was bending down to pick up his gun. Thomas looked up and saw Chester leap over a fallen soldier and run towards the dog.

"He's been hit!" Chris yelled.

"Fall back, fall back!" someone shouted.

"Blue, Blue!" Thomas yelled as he started towards the dog.

"Fall back!" the order came again.

"Blue!" Thomas yelled. Chris grabbed his arm holding Thomas tight to prevent him from moving.

"Let go!" Thomas yelled at Chris.

"We have to fall back," Chris shouted as another cannon shell sent more dirt flying into their eyes. Chris coughed several times, then continued, "Chester rescued Blue. He'll be fine."

Thomas turned and looked at Chester who had picked up Blue and put him on his shoulders.

"Alright, alright," Thomas agreed, turning back towards Chris as they began to walk backwards.

Some of the other men were not as calm in their retreat. Thomas noticed proudly that his comrades in the 71st were much more reserved than many of the others. Perhaps the experience at Ball's Bluff had taught them a lesson. As Thomas watched the chaos unfold, more and more Union soldiers turned around and retreated towards the cornfield, some of the men dropping their rifles as they ran while others were shot in the backs by a stray bullet or some other projectile.

"Nice day for an ambush," a voice from behind them shouted. Thomas and Chris turned to see Chester running behind them, carrying Blue across his shoulders.

"Blue!" Thomas shouted. "Are you alright, boy?"

Blue lifted his head at the sound of Thomas' voice.

"It'll be alright, boy," Thomas tried to comfort him.

"You think it's an ambush?" Chris responded to Chester's comment.

"What else could it be?" Chester replied. Suddenly his body went flying forward and Thomas and Chris were knocked backwards.

"Blue!" Chris called as he saw the dog flying in the air. A cannon shell must have exploded directly underneath Chester. Thomas, stunned for a moment, was able to lift his head to see Chester lying facedown in the dirt and Chris running towards the dog.

"Let's get out of here!" Chris shouted back to Thomas.

Thomas stood up slowly realizing he had twisted his ankle when he fell. He quickly glanced at his body and thanked God that he had not been wounded.

"C'mon!" Chris shouted as he picked up Blue again and moved away from the woods.

Thomas looked back to see the men retreating towards the woods. It had been another disaster for the regiment. Men killed, wounded and maimed, and nothing gained. No land was taken, no point was made, only more death.

CONFEDERATE SOLDIERS, WHO WERE KILLED ON THE HAGERSTOWN ROAD

Chapter Sixteen

The Change

"He's not going to make it, is he?" Thomas said to Chris once the fighting had ended. It had been a horrible day for the regiment. Over 200 of the 510 men in the regiment were either missing or dead. Chester had been killed. Larry had been killed. Several men had volunteered to find Colonel Wistar among the dead scattered on the field.[1] Many of the officers were also killed or lost and there still was no clear idea what General Lee would do in the morning.

The Confederates had lost badly too. In one section of the battlefield so many men lay piled on top of each other that their blood flowed down the dirt road, coloring it a deep red. Many of the soldiers referred to it as "Bloody Lane."

But Thomas didn't care about that now. All he cared about was his dog. Chris and he had managed to make it back to safety that morning and luckily they did not have to fight any more that day. Unfortunately, Blue had been hit several times, and all the doctors were too busy with the thousands of wounded men to attend to Blue.

---

1. Colonel Wistar was found by these men and taken to a hospital where he eventually recovered.

"I don't think so," Chris finally answered. Blue was lying on the soft grass, breathing heavily and squirming in pain. Chris lifted Blue's head and gave him more water. "He's shot up in several places and he has lost a lot of blood."

Thomas lowered his head and tried to contain himself. He'd seen so much death in the past year: his friends on the bluff, his friends here at Antietam, his dog Alfie, and now Blue. What had he done to deserve this? Would his life be filled with death and destruction wherever he went?

"C'mon, Blue," Chris said softly. He continued to pat the dog's back, being careful to stay away from the wounds. "Try to rest, boy."

Blue kept his head up and looked around as though he refused to simply lay down and die. He sniffed the air and rubbed his nose into Chris's pockets.

"What, what?" Chris asked the dog.

Thomas looked up again and smiled. "He wants your baseball."

"My baseball?" Chris repeated. "Well, I'll be..."

Chris reached his hand into his pocket and pulled out his baseball. Blue's head shot up and he stuck out his tongue.

"Can you believe this?" Chris said to Thomas.

"Throw it up just a little so he can catch it," Thomas suggested.

Chris watched as Blue easily snatched the ball with his jaws.

"Good boy!" Thomas and Chris said in unison.

Blue put his head back down on the ground and let the baseball roll out of his mouth.

"Do it again," Thomas suggested.

"O.K.," Chris agreed. He realized that it was keeping the dog happy and it was certainly better than sitting there sadly waiting for him to die.

Chris tossed the ball up again; Blue caught it and again returned it to the ground.

"Good boy," Chris and Thomas repeated. Thomas rubbed the top of Blue's head.

"One more time," Thomas said. *Maybe the fun will give him enough strength to recover,* he thought to himself.

Chris picked up the ball, tossed it in the air, and Blue caught it. He laid his head down on the ground, but this time the ball stayed in his teeth.

"Blue?" Thomas prompted. "Blue?"

The ball rolled out on its own.

"Blue!" Thomas shouted.

Blue's tongue slumped out of his mouth and his eyes rolled back.

"Blue!" Thomas shouted again as he tightly hugged the dog. "Blue, oh Blue," he sobbed.

Several soldiers from the regiment heard Thomas' weeping and gathered around to stand quietly over Thomas and Blue. No one said a word. A few of them had tears in their eyes as well. It was strange how so few of them cried when a man was lost, yet when the dog died it seemed to be different.

"We need to give him a proper regimental burial," one of them suggested.

"Yeah," three or four of them agreed.

"Think the lieutenant will let us?" another wondered. "We're supposed to be on the ready for another attack."

"Nothing's going to happen now, it's too late."

"Well, let's get started then."

Most of the men went to find spades to dig a grave while Thomas and Chris stayed with the dog. It was weird what an effect Blue had on them. Here in the middle of the war with all this killing, death, and destruction the men were taking the time to bury the dog. Thomas couldn't help thinking as he sat there hugging Blue that he had been more than just their mascot. He had been a friend to them. When they needed an escape from the war, he had been there to play with them. Feeding him, bathing him, and taking care of him had distracted them from army life and given them a little taste of life back home. And last but not least, Blue had been a symbol of their innocence. Blue didn't care about politics, slavery, constitutions, or states. He only cared about running, playing, and having fun with his friends in the regiment. When the soldiers played with Blue they forgot all of these things as well. With his death, the innocence of life was lost, nothing remained but war and fighting and death. The loss was almost more than Thomas could bare.

"C'mon, Thomas," Harold, the soldier who had organized the grave detail said. "It's time."

As Thomas headed towards the grave he reflected on this incident and realized how much he had changed. Throughout the battle he never feared for himself. Of course, he did not want to die, but he did not feel the need to run away as he had in the past. During the battle when Blue went down, he could only think about getting the dog to safety. And now, with Blue gone, he didn't feel alone and afraid. He felt somehow strengthened by his resolve to press on. He would not let Blue and his friends die in vain. He would make his uncle and cousins and brother and sisters proud of him. If he ever ran again it would be towards a battle, not away from it.

It's funny, Thomas thought finally. *I almost feel good.*

Epilogue

Antietam

Thomas had won. He had stood his ground. He hadn't run.

The Union had won. They had stood their ground. They had stopped General Lee.

Although thousands of men were killed by both sides during the battle, the Union had managed to stop General Lee's invasion of the North. Lee and his Army of Northern Virginia recrossed the Potomac River and the North was safe for another day.

The Battle of Antietam (called Sharpsburg by the Confederates) on September 17, 1862, turned out to be the bloodiest single day in American history with more than 26,000 men killed, wounded, or missing. In the cornfield that Thomas had to cross, General Hooker later claimed: "In the time that I am writing, every stalk of corn in the northern and greater part of the field was cut as closely as could have been done with a knife, and the slain lay in rows precisely as they had stood in their ranks a few moments before. It was never my fortune to witness a more bloody, dismal battlefield."[1]

---

1. Linda Ervin, *The Battle of Antietam.*

Militarily, the battle was a draw. No ground had been gained and both armies would survive to fight another day. For the Northerners, however, and especially for Thomas many things had changed. Finally, the North could claim that it did not lose a battle. Just as Thomas had finally stood his ground and refused to run, so too had the Union army. Lee had been turned back. In addition to that, England and France decided to stay out of the war, in part, because of the results of Antietam. The Confederacy was all alone.

Perhaps more important to Thomas and his family was that President Lincoln issued the Emancipation Proclamation on September 22, 1862, 5 days after the Battle of Antietam. The war had been changed from a war to restore the Union to a war to end slavery. The abolitionists cheered.

Unfortunately, the story of the War Between the States was far from over. The South was still quite capable of fighting and it showed no desire to surrender. Although Lincoln had freed the slaves, he had only freed the slaves in the Confederacy, where he had no power. For most of the slaves trapped in the South, their lives did not change. The commanding Union general at Antietam, General George B. McClellan, had failed to achieve a decisive victory even with a copy of Lee's plans in his hands. After failing to follow the Confederate army and allowing them to escape, McClellan was fired by President Lincoln. President Lincoln continued to search for a new general to lead the Army of the Potomac. The Southern generals continued to confidently lead a powerful, loyal group of veterans willing to fight for their cause. The Civil War would be a long war.

The Emancipation Proclamation
An Abridged Transcription

By the President of the United States of America:
A Proclamation.

*Whereas, on the twenty-second day of September, in the year of our Lord **one thousand eight hundred and sixty-two**, a proclamation was issued by the President of the United States, containing, among other things, the following, to wit:*

***That** on the first day of January, in the year of our Lord one thousand eight hundred and sixty-three, **all persons held as slaves** within any State or designated part of a State, the people whereof shall then be in rebellion against the United States, **shall be then, thenceforward, and forever free;** and the executive government of the United States, including the military and naval authority thereof, will recognize and maintain the freedom of such persons and will do no act or acts to repress such persons, or any of them, in any efforts they may make for their actual freedom....*

***And I further declare** and make known **that such persons [freed slaves]** of suitable condition **will be received into the armed service of the United States** to garrison forts, positions, stations, and other places, and to man vessels of all sorts in said service.*

And upon this act, sincerely believed to be an act of justice, warranted by the Constitution upon military necessity, I invoke the considerate judgment of mankind and the gracious favor of Almighty God....

Done at the City of Washington, this first day of January, in the year of our Lord one thousand eight

*hundred and sixty three, and of the Independence of
the United States of America the eighty-seventh.*

*By the President: ABRAHAM LINCOLN
WILLIAM H. SEWARD, Secretary of State.*

PRESIDENT LINCOLN, WRITING THE PROCLAMATION OF FREEDOM [*sic*], JANUARY 1, 1863

National Archives

PREVIEW

LOOK FOR THIS SCENE IN BOOK FIVE OF THE YOUNG HEROES OF HISTORY SERIES: *NO GIRLS ALLOWED*

The soldier stared at Mary waiting to see her reaction.

"A girl!" Mary repeated. "But...but...how...how...," Mary mumbled.

"Private Lynn Rhodes, 7th Maine, at your service," Lynn said with a slight smile. She was relieved to finally tell someone. After all it had been over a year since she and Daniel, her brother, had joined the Union army. She had grown very tired of the secrecy and the pretense of the lies and the half-truths. She had tired of the girl jokes, pretending to think they were funny. If she hadn't been concerned for the boys in her unit she might have left a long time ago.

"Lynn?" Mary managed to repeat. "But...how did you..."

"Join up?" Lynn finished the sentence for her. "It was easy. I just cut my hair, taped down my chest, and here I am." She smiled again with pride that she had been able to hide her secret for so long.

"But how did you keep it a secret?" Mary wondered aloud. She still couldn't believe what she was seeing.

145

"It wasn't so hard," Lynn answered. "I'm sure you realize how rarely soldiers bathe. Between that and having my twin brother in the same company, it was a cinch to fool everyone."

"Twin brother?" Mary repeated.

"Yeah," Lynn answered. "His name's Daniel Rhodes."

"But why would you want to do this?" Mary gasped. Despite what Lynn had done to camouflage her true identity, Mary still couldn't believe that a woman would pretend to be a man. What good would it do? What would she prove?

"To get involved, of course," Lynn responded quickly. She was surprised and a little annoyed that Mary would be asking her this question. "Isn't that why you're here?"

"Y-yes, but..."

"But what?" Lynn charged. "I don't belong in a uniform? I should be content taking care of the wounded and cleaning their mess?"

"This is an important job!" Mary shouted. Other soldiers lying in their beds, looked at her.

"Yeah, yeah, fine," Lynn whispered as she motioned with her hands to be quiet. "Whatever you say. Just keep it down, O.K.?"

Mary nodded slightly, still not sure what she was going to do with Lynn, who obviously had broken the rules. It was only a matter of time before she was discovered by the authorities. Although Mary did not agree with Lynn's actions, Mary respected her for her bravery; yet, she did not want to be the one to snitch on her.

"So?" Lynn charged sensing a weakness in Mary. "Are you going to turn me in?"

BIBLIOGRAPHY

Alexander Cartwright and the Knickerbockers. Baseball Before Professionalism. Http://www.geocities.com/ Colosseum/Bleachers/5573/knicks.htm; June 9, 2000.

Battle of Antietam, The. Peterborough, N.H.: Cobblestone Publishing Co., October 1997.

Billings, John D. *Hardtack and Coffee.* Boston: George M. Smith & Co., 1887.

Boyer, Paul S., and others. *The Enduring Vision: A History of the American People.* Lexington, Mass.: D. C. Heath, 1990.

Catton, Bruce. *Hayfoot, Strawfoot: The Civil War Soldier.* New York: American Heritage, April 1957.

Davis, Burke. *Boys in the Civil War.* Http://www. civilwarhome.com/boysinwar.htm; February 10, 2000.

Ervin, Linda. *The Battle of Antietam.* Http://www. rockingham.k12.va.us/ems/The Battle of Antietam/ Antietam.htm.

Jones, Wilbur D. *Excerpts of Special Orders No. 191,* without illustrations, from *Giants in the Cornfield: The 27th Indiana Infantry.* Http://www.aeb.com/ brdowney/so191.html; February 10, 2000.

Lash, Gary. *The Battle of Antietam.* Http://www. geocities.com/Athens/Academy/1216/ antietam.html; May 31, 2000.

———. *The Battle of Ball's Bluff.* Http://www. geocities.com/Athens/Academy/1216/ ballsblu.html; February 10, 2000.

———. *Edward Baker's California Regiment.* Http:// www.geocities.com/Athens/Academy/1216/ 71stpenn.html; June 15, 1998.

McCutcheon, Marc. *Everyday Life in the 1800s.* Cincinnati: Writer's Digest Books, 1993.

McPherson, James M. *Battle Cry of Freedom.* New York: Oxford University Press, 1988.

Murphy, Jim. *The Boys' War.* New York: Clarion Books, 1990.

O'Shea, Richard, and David Greenspan. *American Heritage: Battle Maps of the Civil War.* New York: Smithmark, 1992.

Priest, John Michael. *Before Antietam: The Battle for South Mountain.* Shippensburg, Pa.: White Mane Publishing Co., Inc., 1992.

Robertson, James I. *Tenting Tonight: The Civil War Series.* Alexandria, Va.: Time Life Books, 1984.

Taylor, Frank H. *Philadelphia in the Civil War.* Philadelphia: Published by the City, 1913.

Thorp, Dr. A. D. *Volunteers for Glory.* Baltimore: American Literary Press, Inc., 1999.

Waskie, Dr. Andy. Philadelphia and surroundings in 1860s: An e-mail correspondence with the author regarding Grand Army of the Republic Civil War Museum and Library. February 21, 2000.